A PLACE FOR CHRISTMAS

WANDER CREEK BOOK THREE

AMY RUTH ALLEN

CHAPTER 1

*C*onstruction grit did not go well with beige suede ankle boots and dark dress jeans, Abby Barrett decided, shaking her mane of honey-blonde hair to get rid of the drywall dust. She should have accepted the surgical shoe coverings when she had the chance. But they were hideous, and the dull teal green clashed with her outfit. She moved slightly to the left. If she wasn't careful, she figured she might trip over a screwdriver or hammer or skill saw, or some other tool that threatened to tear a gaping hole in her jeans. She was also standing dangerously close to a piece of plywood with splinters poking out the sides, just waiting to snag her silk blouse.

"Why don't you step out of the construction zone," Abby's boyfriend Ken suggested, eyeing the dust on her shoulders. "Either that or put on a hard hat. And it appears you may be slightly overdressed."

Abby gladly followed Ken's suggestion and plopped down on a nearby bar stool that was far enough away from the action that she wouldn't risk a potential wardrobe malfunction. Ken, of course, was dressed in heavy tan canvas pants, work boots, and a black and red plaid shirt. At six-feet, he was effortlessly handsome, with a head of thick sandy blond hair and deep brown eyes.

"You don't know how much I appreciate you doing this for me," Abby said. "There's no way I could get this done without you."

Abby was a successful entrepreneur and businesswoman who, in the strangest manner possible, had inherited a commercial building on Main Street in the small tourist town of Wander Creek in northern Minnesota. Sometimes she felt she was so far north that she could walk to the Canadian border and be in another country in the blink of an eye. Which wasn't that far from the truth.

She looked around the store space and took in all Ken had accomplished in such a brief time. He had generously offered to do the necessary renovations to bring Abby's new retail endeavor, The Book Box, up to code and ready to open for business on Black Friday. Ken had rehabbed the sagging built-in bookshelves that lined the walls, and built new ones, complete with sturdy caster wheels so they could easily be rolled out of the way to make room for the requisite folding chairs that would certainly be needed for author book signings and readings. The sales counter near the back of the store had also needed a refresh and he had sanded it down until the original oak shone through. He showed Abby how to paint on a layer of shellack to seal up the wood and create a sturdy and beautiful finish. That time, she had been smart enough to wear old clothes and tie her hair into a top bun.

And although Abby had a full-time job running her first retail endeavor, the Paper Box, she and Ken stayed up way into the night several times to paint the walls of the Book Box a cheerful buttery yellow with rich cream-colored baseboards and crown molding. The pair hung new curtains and carefully arranged the various display tables and shelves. They were doing their best to make sure the place would sparkle on opening day.

Dennis Grey, the previous owner, had kept the bookstore in rather good order, but he had not really updated anything for thirty years. That was part of the bookstore's charm—when it belonged to Dennis. But now that it belonged to Abby—well, it needed to reflect *her* particular sensibilities and vision. The last bit of the renovation had involved Ken tearing out a good-sized section of an old plaster wall on the east side of the building. The plaster was so cracked that it was beyond repair. Ken was pounding it with a large sledgehammer and the plaster was crumbling under his efforts, exposing the underlying wood strips that he would also rip out, making way for a layer of modern insulation and drywall.

"Fifteen more minutes and you can invite me upstairs for a glass of wine," Ken said, letting the chunks of old plaster fall onto the tarp he had spread over the floor. "It's been a while since we've put our feet up together and just talked."

Abby felt a pang in her stomach because she was feeling more than a little guilty that she had not spent much time with Ken recently. And on purpose. She had a good excuse, of course. And kind, amiable Ken understood how busy she was, running a successful business and fast-tracking the opening of a second one. *Okay, that's my excuse.* Dear Ken. But she had purposely been avoiding talking with him very much, or more to the point, trying to avoid *him* talking to *her*. But she absolutely needed Ken to help with the renovation. *I hope I'm not taking advantage of him. At least not too much.*

Ken had even turned over the daily operations of his highly successful outdoor adventure store, Northwoods, to his assistant manager, just so he would have more time to help Abby complete the work in just one week. That was a big deal for Ken, having grown his business up over the years into one of the most sought-after and respected outdoor adventure stores in the Midwest.

I don't deserve him, Abby thought miserably.

Abby simply could not get out of her head the image of Ken and Marcus—Marcus being her good friend Mona's beau— passing a black velvet jewelry box between them a few weeks earlier in the parlor of the elegant and exclusive Wander Inn. It was Mona's birthday party, and Ken and Marcus were huddled in a corner, talking with their heads together, admiring something in the small box like schoolboys. The box obviously contained an engagement ring. *What else could it have been?* Abby had looked away for just an instant to see if anyone else was watching the scene. But when she turned back, the black velvet jewelry box was gone, and Ken and Marcus were just standing there chatting amiably, both men with their hands in their front pants pockets.

And what, exactly, was she supposed to do with that? She loved Ken, but after the horrible fallout of her first marriage, Abby wasn't sure if she was anywhere near ready to take the plunge again. *I really hope he doesn't ask me to marry him. At least not right now.*

Even though she was a grown woman, Abby had taken the very immature route of avoiding Ken as much as possible, and only spending time with him when she had carefully calculated that it would be absolutely the worst time for any man to propose to the woman he loved. It was all she could think to do.

"What the heck?!" Ken exclaimed. "There's something in here, behind the wall." His arm was hidden behind the crumbling plaster.

"Oh, no," Abby squealed. She instinctively drew her knees up to her chest to avoid being attacked by whatever four—or maybe twenty-legged—creepy creature that was about to scramble out of the wall and devour them both. "What is it? Is it alive? Don't tell me it's a snake. Is it a huge spider? Or a bat?"

Ken looked up at her grinning. "Relax. It's not a living crea- ture. It feels like a … I can just about reach it. Got it!"

Abby watched as Ken withdrew his arm and held up a small canvas, maybe a foot square. Painted upon it was a man in

4

profile. "How do you like them apples?" he said, gently brushing dirt and debris from the painting with the back of his hand. "I'm pretty sure there's another one in there. I'm going back in." He handed the first canvas to Abby, who was now standing beside Ken, no longer worried about being eaten alive by a horde of creepy critters.

As Ken fished around for more treasure, Abby held the small painting up in front of her. Although it was dusty from years of being forgotten and neglected, Abby could tell instantly that it was exquisitely done, clearly painted by a very talented professional artist.

The painting was done in acrylic paint, and depicted a youngish man reading a book, relaxing on a window seat surrounded by pillows. Abby automatically glanced up and across the sales floor to the front window. Then she glanced back at the painting. No similarities between the windows.

"Here's another one," Ken said, presenting Abby with another canvas of the same size. "That's all of them. Give me a few more minutes and I'll have all these wooden strips removed and all I'll have left to install the insulation and hang the drywall. I know you're in a hurry, so why don't I just mount the drywall and we can push one of those tall bookshelves up against the wall to hide it. Nobody will be the wiser. I'll finish the joints later. Then we can go have that drink at your place."

Abby was barely listening. "Hmmm," she said, as she took the second painting from Ken.

In this second painting, what looked to be the same man was leaning against a tree, vibrant with colorful fall leaves, in a beautiful meadow, his eyes closed and an open book resting on his chest, as if he had fallen asleep while reading.

As it turned out, pulling out the last bit of plaster took a bit longer than Ken had anticipated. It was after ten before he finished, and Abby was helping him straighten up and put away his tools.

"Sorry, sweetie, but I have a sunrise ATV tour to lead tomorrow. I've got to prep some gear and get to bed. Raincheck on the nightcap?"

Abby kissed him lightly on the lips. "Of course. We'll do it another time, and I'll even make those gouda cheese straws you like so much."

Ken gave a thumbs up and let himself out the front door, and the little bell the previous owner had attached to signal the comings and goings of customers jingled as he exited.

Abby grabbed her purse and the paintings and headed out the front door, locking it behind her, and proceeded directly next door to the Paper Box. She wished she had remembered to leave the front light on. She fumbled with her keys and the paintings, but finally managed to let herself in, and she made her way up the stairs to her small apartment.

It was always a relief to come home. She loved her light, airy apartment with its twelve-foot ceilings. The living and dining spaces were one large combined open space decorated with neutral tones. After work in the winter, she loved to cozy up on the light grey couches that flanked the fireplace and rest her feet on the oversized ottoman that served as a coffee table.

She dropped her purse on the kitchen island, then walked over and placed the paintings side by side on her long farmhouse-style dining room table. *The colors are unbelievably beautiful.* Abby loved the neutral tones, the muted yellow splashes of light and the faded blues, which contrasted so gracefully with the vibrant fall colors of orange, red, and yellow.

She turned the paintings over to inspect the backs. The canvases were obviously done manually, rather than mass-produced. The staples that held the canvas to the frame displayed a hint of rust and were slightly akimbo, not in the straight line one would expect from a machine produced canvas.

Abby flipped them back over and inspected them carefully, searching for evidence of a signature, eventually having to forcefully wrest herself away from them, as exciting and mysterious as they were. *I've got to focus on tomorrow.* Tomorrow was going to be a big day. Carmen was coming. Everything was falling into place.

That night, filled with excitement for the next day, Abby struggled to fall asleep. When she finally drifted off, she dreamed of the man in the meadow.

~

*A*bby woke up early the next morning, thrilled that she and Ken had made such good progress toward opening the Book Box. And best of all, Carmen was coming! Abby dressed in her best jeans and a scarlet sweater set. She looked out the window that overlooked Main Street. No snow yet, thank goodness. Winter came early in northern Minnesota. There had been a few flurries, but it wasn't here in full force yet. Abby brought out her peep-toe patent leather heels. *Okay, maybe the peep-toe is a little overdoing it. But the fact remains there's no snow on the ground. And it's not even supposed to rain.*

It was Sunday and the Paper Box was closed. Abby descended the stairs from her apartment onto the sales floor, sailing past the racks of greeting cards, beautiful displays of wrapping paper, eco-friendly gifts, designer office supplies, and much more, and dashed out of the front door. It was just a few steps to the Book Box directly next door. She was pumped with adrenaline on the idea that in a few short weeks, the Book Box would have customers. Customers with money in their pockets. She was becoming a serial entrepreneur. Fumbling with her keys a bit— her hands were shaking from anticipation, not the cold November air—she unlocked the door and stepped inside. It was eerily quiet. She flipped on the lights, flooding the sales room with a splash of pale yellow. With a flourish, she ripped the protective sheets off the display tables, which she had begun to decorate and stock with the inventory she had already ordered. She slowly tore the butcher paper from the bookshelves. Ken had taped them up to keep any construction dust from settling on the books. Abby had purposefully held back on decorating for the holidays, knowing that Carmen would want to put her own special touch on the place.

The thought of owning a second business in Wander creek hadn't occurred to her until the day she was browsing around Pages bookstore, and Dennis, the pleasant owner, told her he was preparing to retire, and the store would soon be for sale. She made the decision instantly, going from zero to sixty in the blink, literally, of her eyes.

It would be a perfect fit! she thought to herself that day, *and I could call it the Book Box.* She had no idea how she would run two businesses at the same time. It did help that the two shops were side-by-side. But it wasn't like she could run from store to store every time a customer went into the other. But she would figure all that out in time.

That very evening she had called Carmen, her old friend and boss at the Paperie boutique in Minneapolis, where Abby had worked after her husband—ex-husband now, thank goodness—left her penniless. She was thrilled to learn that Carmen had recently decided to sell the store she had owned for thirty years and was looking around for new opportunities. The timing was perfect. Carmen would come to Wander Creek and manage the Book Box on a trial basis, and Abby would provide her housing in the apartment above the store.

It didn't matter to Abby that Carmen didn't know much about running a bookstore. After very successfully operating her upscale and prosperous stationery store, Carmen knew retail, and whatever else she needed she could learn.

Besides, Abby felt like an old hand at this sort of project. She had just done the same thing for the Paper Box. She just needed to find a manager with retail experience, and more importantly, a manager she could trust. Carmen was the first name that occurred to her.

And she was here! When Abby heard the "honk-honk" of a car horn out front, she gave one last look at the interior, admiring how the store was shaping up, and then stepped out the front door to greet her friend, mentor, and hopefully, the permanent manager of the Book Box.

I sure hope she likes it.

"I can't wait for you to show me around," Carmen said, giving Abby a big warm hug as she got out of her bright yellow Mini Cooper.

"Don't you want to settle in first?" Abby asked. Carmen was a five-foot something bundle of energy, always ready to go, today in a light blue leisure suit and matching tennis shoes that somehow had a sparkle to them.

"Let's take my bags up to the apartment and then we'll have a proper look around," Carmen said.

They each grabbed one of Carmen's two substantial luxury suitcases, wheeled them through the store to the staircase off the office in the back, and headed upstairs. Carmen wolf whistled as she ascended the first couple of stairs. "Oooh, I can't wait."

As they lugged the bags up the narrow stairs Abby managed to say breathlessly between straining grunts, "I hope this is going to be okay for you. I rented the furniture, so we can take it back if you don't like it."

What she really meant was, *I can take it back if you hate managing the Book Box and hate Wander Creek and hate your life here and move back to Minneapolis.*

"And I brought you plenty of really nice linens from my apartment."

Abby opened the door at the top of the stairs and the pair stepped into the apartment. Abby tried to see the space through Carmen's eyes, knowing full well Carmen's permanent home was a very spacious and beautifully decorated high-rise condominium in downtown Minneapolis. A smallish apartment above a bookstore in a tiny tourist town—well, that might take some getting used to.

I should have decorated this place better, Abby thought, chastising herself for not even bringing over some throw pillows from her extensive collection. *Or plants. Plants would have given a nice pop of color. Or flowers. Oh well. Too late now.*

Carmen dropped her suitcase to the floor with a relieved "uff-dah," and turned to face Abby. Then she glanced around quickly, and simply said, "This will be fine. I wasn't expecting the Ritz Carlton, and it looks like I'll have everything I need. Besides, I plan to spend most of my waking hours in the store or the office. I'll only be up here to sleep and eat." She pinched Abby's cheek. "Now let's get back downstairs to my bookstore."

Abby had turned up the heat before Carmen's arrival and the small store was cozy and warm. The only thing that could have made it more perfect was if there was a cozy fireplace next to the reading nook towards the back of the store by the sales counter, and maybe even some warm mulled wine. Abby thought that she should install a pretty fireplace mantle over a nice set of gas logs. There was so much she could do, and she was brimming with excitement, but she had to remind herself that for now, Carmen was in charge of the store. Abby had promised to give her free reign. *But who would ever say no to a cozy fireplace in Northern Minnesota?*

Carmen strode slowly around the store, unhurriedly taking everything in, seemingly one inch at a time. Her eyes landed on every display, bookshelf, every sign on every section of books. After she had toured the whole store, she wound up at a display table near the front door. On it Abby had arranged an assortment of giftboxes made up just for booklovers. Staring at the display with her chin resting in her right hand, Carmen said, "I like it."

Abby was sincerely hoping she would get Carmen's nod of

approval. "You mean you like that display? Or the store?" Abby asked.

"Both," Carmen replied smiling. "I like both. Now let me get settled in and get my sea legs. You skedaddle and I'll see you tomorrow."

"Okay, but don't forget the welcome dinner at The Wander Inn tomorrow night," Abby reminded her friend. "It's Mona's way of settling you into Wander Creek in style!"

CHAPTER 2

When Abby entered the Book Box the next morning at eight, the store was brightly lit, and butcher paper was taped over the panes of glass in the bay window, blocking the view of passersby. *Carmen must have done that.*

Having heard Abby enter, Carmen called, "Yooh, hooh, I'm in the back."

Abby followed the voice, walking through what looked like a fully stocked store.

"Did you work all day yesterday? Or stay up all night?" she asked Carmen, a look of surprise on her face. "This place looks amazing." She placed a paper cup of coffee on Carmen's small and practical IKEA desk and sipped her own. "Please don't tell me you really stayed up all night. You'll get burned out before we even open," Abby laughed.

"No worries," Carmen responded cheerily. "For years I've gotten by on five hours of sleep a night. It's a habit I can't break, but it sometimes does come in handy when I have a lot of work to do. Here, let me show you around."

Abby followed Carmen obediently. The two had discussed the potential overlap of inventory between the two stores, and while all the profits went to the same place, Abby was adamant that each store offer unique inventory.

Carmen had brought all of the book-related stock from her old stationery store with her.

"How did you get all this in your Mini?" Abby asked, twirling around to get a three-hundred-and-sixty-degree view.

"Experience," Carmen said.

Abby was impressed with what Carmen had done.

"Wow," Abby said delightedly. "You even brought new stock to sell. How much do I owe you?"

"Nothing. I couldn't help myself. While I hate to see any store go out of business, this sweet little bookstore in St. Paul was selling everything at cost. I felt it was a good business decision. I arranged for it to be delivered yesterday. I was hoping you weren't going to see the delivery truck in the alley. I guess you didn't."

Canvas bags and t-shirts with quotes by famous authors hung next to coffee cups sporting images of other famous authors. It was an English major's dream. Carmen had strategically arranged a variety of attractive book ends, little book lights, reading journals, book weights to keep pages from turning in the wind, and so much more. Everything was spectacular, and nothing appeared to duplicate the inventory of the Paper Box. Abby was thrilled. She had been worried about hiring a friend and former boss, but looking around the shop, and seeing Carmen's vision mirror her own, Abby knew she had made the right choice.

"Carmen, this is perfect. It's exactly what I hoped for. Thank you for getting it done so quicky. I know it was a lot of work, but we need to be ready to open on Black Friday." Abby stopped and the two women shared a laugh. "I guess I don't have to tell you that."

"I also have started researching authors from the region. I think that would be a good place to start with doing author readings," Carmen advised.

"Planning ahead. I like that," said Abby, who was a compulsive planner herself. "So what's next? Everything looks done!"

"There's a lot to pull together still. I'm leaning toward rearranging some of the tables, and I want to take a lot of photos and post on social media. And there's the front window display," she added mischievously, a twinkle in her eye.

Abby clapped her hand and gave a little happy dance. "My favorite part. What do you have in mind?"

"How about we regroup on the window display in about a week," Carmen suggested. "I can't wait to show you what I've come up with. I have to work it out logistically still, but you'll love it."

And Abby knew she would.

≈

That evening Abby got a text from Ken. "Here," it simply said. Abby bounded down the stairs and out the front door of the Paper Box, locking it behind her, and saw Ken's truck parked at the curb. Ken stretched across the cab of the truck and opened the door for her, and Abby scrambled into the front passenger seat and gave Ken a quick kiss.

"Hi!" Abby said cheerfully, greeting her friend Jessica Lake, seated in the back. Blonde, petite, and perky, Jessica owned the Life and Style boutique on the other side of Main Street from Abby's stores.

"Let's get this party started," Jessica sang. "I can't wait to see what we're having for dinner. I'm starving. Isn't it nice that Ken picked me up? I love being escorted by handsome men."

"I was out her way," Ken said, "so I took the initiative and swung by and picked her up."

"How nice of you," Abby said, adding another hashmark in the

14

"pros" column in the imaginary pros and cons list she kept for Ken. She hated that she had started doing that. But now that she had started, she couldn't stop.

Abby saw movement in the side view mirror, and a moment later Carmen was standing on the sidewalk smiling at her. Jessica saw her, too, opened the truck door, and beckoned for Carmen to join her in the back seat as she slid over to make room. Carmen climbed in, and Ken waited for further instructions.

After a bit of small talk, Abby proposed to the foursome, "You know what? It's such a beautiful night. We should walk to the Inn."

As they strolled westward down Main Street, Abby took in the splendor of Wander Creek.

She gazed at each storefront's decorations as they passed by, knowing in her heart that everyone was trying their best not to be outdone by her. *Which is usually the case,* she joked with herself.

The November night air was fresh and crisp, hovering around the freezing mark, and Main Street was bustling with both tourists and locals, darting to and fro, intent on finding that perfect Christmas gift in one of Wander Creek's unique shops before they closed for the evening. *I should have kept the store open a bit later,* Abby thought. She breathed the fresh air in deeply, glanced at Ken, at Jessica, and at Carmen. *How did I get so lucky to have such great friends?* she thought to herself.

Abby had been in Wander Creek long enough to pick out the groups of deer hunting widows happily walking the streets, usually fortified by wine, whose husbands were on the hunting trip of a lifetime with some popular north woods deer hunting guide who knew all the best spots in the Superior National Forest. Abby waved and smiled at such a group headed in the opposite direction. Ken managed to interject that his establishment catered to people like their husbands, but Abby was not surprised that the wives were not interested in the least.

Those hunting widows had spent a small fortune in Abby's store, and she was grateful for them. She was also grateful for the day trippers from Duluth, who represented a significant portion of the tourists. She was humbled by everyone that entered the doors of the Paper Box and left with merchandise.

Soon Abby's group stood before the beautiful wooden front door of the Wander Inn. Built in the 1920s, the large building took up the equivalent space of an entire city block and was solidly constructed from stone with rich brown cedar shake shingles. White columns and window trim shone under the landscape lights. Mona and her staff had decorated the front portico and doors beautifully, with lush greens, gold ribbons, and ornaments galore.

Abby turned to Carmen and asked, "Don't you just love this place?"

"It's beautiful, that's for sure. Can't wait to see the inside."

Before anyone could raise their arm to push the door open, it swung open, seemingly of its own accord.

"Greetings all," said Mona, politely beckoning the group to enter. "Welcome to the Wander Inn!" she said, even though Carmen was the only member of the group who had never been there before.

Mona was an imposing figure, standing almost six-feet tall in her designer high heels, which made her an entire foot taller than Carmen. Mona was impeccably dressed in a deep red wrap dress and her ash blonde bob, as always, looked as if it never moved. She practically dripped with gold jewelry studded with pearls and diamonds.

Just a typical evening at the Wander Inn for Mona Sixsmith, Abby thought, putting her arm through Carmen's and saying, "Mona, I would like you to officially meet Carmen, the angel who saved me when I desperately needed saving."

Abby wasn't sure, but it seemed to her that Mona hesitated a bit before holding out her hand to shake Carmen's, which she did without much conviction.

"It's so nice to meet you," Mona said, also without much conviction. "I've been an angel many times myself. Even to Abby here."

What the heck? Abby thought to herself.

Abby was glad when they were all seated at the beautifully set table in a small private dining room. Mona had put out fancy place cards, and she had reserved the head of the table for herself and placed Carmen directly opposite her at the foot. She had placed Abby and Ken in the two chairs on the right side of the table with Abby in the chair closest to her. In the two chairs on the left side of the table she had placed her boyfriend Marcus Fairchild, who had not yet arrived, and Jessica Lake.

Ken and Jessica were both skilled at small talk, and they kept the conversation light and comfortable. Abby noticed that Mona had spared no expense for this occasion. Gorgeous freshly cut flowers adorned the room, and although Abby had dined at the Inn many times, she had never seen this particular fine china.

Mona must have noticed Abby admiring it because she said to Abby, "It's beautiful, isn't it? It's Wedgwood. This style is very rare. It was made in the late nineteenth century. Only the best for you, my dear." She reached across the table and patted Abby's hand.

And then as an afterthought she faced Carmen and said, "And only the best for you, too, of course."

It was completely obvious to Abby that Mona didn't mean a word of what she just said. Whatever was going on between her two mentors, she didn't like it. She was relieved to see Telly coming through the door. And he had alcohol. Abby could never tell how old he was. Somedays he looked like he could be forty, and others he looked sixty-ish. No matter how old he was, what never wavered was his unflappable and deep devotion to Mona, who had not only given him a job as the Inn's chef but had set him up in one of the tiny houses at the back of the Inn's property.

Telly was very tall and thin, with a strangely handsome but gaunt face and mop of unruly dark hair. And he always looked very distinguished in his chef's jacket, checkered pants, and white chef's hat.

Telly took a place behind Mona and slightly to her right, and standing tall, he simply said, "Greetings all."

Mona stood quickly to introduce Telly to Carmen. She reached over and took Telly's hand in hers. Abby had never seen Mona actually hold Telly's hand before. *That's a little weird.*

"Carmen," Mona began, "may I present to you the backbone of the Wander Inn, Telluride Simmons. Telly is what we call him. I found him in a desperate situation." She turned to Telly and asked, "You were living in your van, were you not?"

This has got to be embarrassing for poor Telly, Abby thought to herself as Mona blabbered on with more detail about Telly's story than Abby had ever heard. And more details than were appropriate for a dinner party.

When Mona finished the story, she did it with a flourish. "So, I guess you could say I was *his* guardian angel."

"She speaks the truth," was Telly's simple response. He beamed at Mona adoringly and obviously wasn't in the least bit embarrassed.

Telly beckoned for Mona to sit down and then skillfully grabbed the bottle of chilled Prosecco he had prepositioned on the buffet table, and strolled gracefully to the foot of the table, and stood beside Carmen.

I could swear I just saw Carmen's eyes light up, Abby thought.

Telly extended his free hand toward Carmen, and when she pushed her chair back a bit to stand up, he said, "Please, remain seated."

Telly shook Carmen's hand, holding on to it a bit longer than one might expect, and Abby noticed they were both smiling brightly. With Carmen's hand fully but softly in his grip, Telly said, "Welcome to Wander Creek, and especially to the Wander Inn."

"Thank you so much," Carmen said softly, obviously totally enamored with Telly.

And then Telly said, "As our guest of honor, may I pour you the evening's first glass?" Telly filled Carmen's glass, then he returned to the head of the table to fill Mona's. He served Abby next, then Jessica, then Ken.

Everybody turned their heads at once when there was a knock on the door frame of the parlor. "Sorry I'm late," said a distinguished older gentleman as he entered the room. Abby wondered if Ken would look as good as Marcus when he was in his seventies.

Does Marcus have an odd look on his face? Abby wondered. *He looks like the cat who swallowed the canary.* Did this have anything to do with that little black jewelry box she had witnessed being passed between Ken and Marcus that recent night at the Inn? Or was she just being paranoid?

Marcus was no taller than five-foot-ten, and his aristocratic appearance perfectly matched his status as a multi-national media mogul. He was the kind of man who had enough confidence that it didn't matter to him if his girlfriend stood a few inches taller. Marcus was Mona's beau, and probably the only person Mona had ever met who had more money than she did. Except for the Russian oligarch. After Mona's husband had passed away, she had inherited an English castle, which she promptly sold to the oligarch much to her in-laws' consternation, as they naturally wanted it to remain in their family. But Mona was simply getting her revenge for how horribly they had treated her over the years, never really accepting an American "commoner" into their highbrow British high-society circle. Abby liked Marcus because he obviously adored Mona.

I wonder if Marcus adores her enough to propose, Abby wondered, admonishing herself for being paranoid again. There could have been anything in that jewelry box. Marcus' sister, Elise Winters, lived close by in a cabin in the woods just on the other side of the creek. Maybe it was her birthday and Marcus just happened to have the box with him and had said, "Hey Ken, you want to see the present I just bought for my sister?"

That was unlikely, Abby decided, as Telly began serving the first course, a thick corn chowder soup topped with skinless grape tomatoes, prosciutto crisped to perfection, mozzarella here and there, all topped with fresh basil and cracked pepper.

It was a work of art and Abby knew she would be moaning with delight when she tasted the first delicious spoonful. She was right.

Next came an arugula green salad, followed by the tenderest pork tenderloin Abby had ever eaten. It was accompanied by perfectly roasted cauliflower, with a fresh herb garnish, and a reduction sauce that Abby wanted to lick off the plate.

When dessert was served, Abby couldn't help but notice that Telly served Carmen the first lemon bar, replete with a slightly more than appropriate amount of cream cheese icing—more than everyone else would get.

"Oh, lemon bars are my absolute favorite," Carmen lied. "How did you know?"

Telly couldn't help but smile, and Abby could have sworn she heard a barely audible chuckle from him.

After some back-and-forth conversation and small talk about how delicious the food was, how beautifully it was prepared, and a group decision was made that Telly really ought to appear on a cooking show, Mona turned to Carmen and said sweetly, "I hope the food wasn't too rich for you, dear."

Carmen smiled back, just as sweetly, as in saccharine sweet, Abby decided.

"Oh, not at all. I'm a bit of a foodie myself. My palate is very, how shall I say, cosmopolitan? Worldly?" she said, still smiling a little too sweetly. "And there are so many restaurants in Minneapolis. It seems like there's a new one popping up every week. I've been to practically all of them. At least, to all of the best ones. And the food trucks. Some of their menus are practically gourmet."

Carmen paused when, as if on cue, Telly appeared at her side and refreshed her Prosecco. The two exchanged a warm smile, and Abby could tell Mona was not impressed. Not impressed with Carmen, and not impressed with Telly's interest in her.

Carmen then continued, looking directly at Mona, "Perhaps one day you will have the good fortune to try my steak pizzaiola. Italian food is my specialty. I usually make it with porterhouse or ribeye. And of course, all fresh garlic and basil goes without saying. And I make my own bread. It's exquisite."

"Oh, how sweet," Mona responded, and then immediately changed the subject to her fabulous florist who flew in flowers from around the world just for her.

Mona and Carmen continued to make little digs at each other throughout the rest of the dinner. Abby thought they were acting like children, and was glad when Telly removed the dessert dishes.

When Mona offered coffee to her guests, Abby politely declined for her foursome, making the excuse that Carmen wanted to get an early start in the morning at the Book Box.

"Lovely idea," Mona agreed. "I'm sure she'll need it."

Ken and Abby exchanged glances and raised eyebrows. They were surely thinking the same thing.

Uh-oh.

⁓

As the foursome made its way back down Main Street toward

the shops, Abby experienced a feeling of unease somewhere near the pit of her stomach. The season of joy was upon them, but what she felt gathering in her heart, despite the decorations and the prospect of falling snow, was a sense of dread. What had come over Carmen and Mona? It was as if her two dear friends had experienced some terrible encounter in their past. Their dislike for each other was obvious and palpable. Abby had never seen anything like it, and she did not like it one bit.

When they got to the Book Box, Ken and Jessica said their goodbyes, and Ken headed out in his truck to drop Jessica off and head home himself.

Abby and Carmen were standing on the sidewalk when Abby turned to Carmen and said, "I couldn't help but notice that … whatever it was, between you and Mona. Do you want to talk about it?"

Always the straight shooter, Carmen did not pretend she didn't know what Abby was talking about. She sighed heavily and wrapped her arms around herself to stave off the cold.

"I suppose we should," she said. "But not here. I'm about to freeze to the ground and then you'd need to find another manager."

Abby let them into the Paper Box and led the way to the back of the store and up the stairs. As they emerged into the apartment, Abby immediately kicked off her suede ankle boots with the three-inch heels and sank into the comfortable couch.

"Why do I wear these?" she whined. "They always end up pinching and torturing me."

"You wear them," Carmen said smiling and taking a seat on the comfy chair next to the fireplace, "because they look good on you, and you know it."

Abby rubbed her feet, wishing she could take off her tights and jump right into her lounge pants. It had been a long day and the strange and exhausting dinner at Mona's had worn her out. Abby waited for her friend and mentor to speak.

When Carmen remained silent, Abby took the lead. "So, that tension between you and Mona that was so thick you could cut it with a knife—what was that all about?" she asked.

Carmen sighed again. "I don't know what happened. Wait, let me back up." Carmen shifted in her chair and tucked her legs under her. "Have you ever taken an instant dislike to a person for seemingly no reason?" she asked. "Because I haven't. Not before tonight that is."

Abby thought back to the people she had known as a wealthy socialite in her former life. There were plenty of unsavory people she had to put up with for various charities and parties, but never someone she disliked on first sight.

"Not that I can recall," she said. "And you'd think that would be something I would remember."

"It's a strange feeling," Carmen said quietly. "It's almost as if something I couldn't control came over me. And every time she said something I had to respond. It was like a tennis match of words, and we were playing to the bitter end, game, set, and match. And instead of points, we were fighting for the last word."

"Which Mona got," Abby observed, laughing and trying to lighten the mood.

"She sure did," Carmen said, only half-smiling. "For now."

Soon after, Abby let Carmen out the front door and watched to make sure she got safely into the Book Box before she locked the Paper Box door. Abby hurried up the stairs and changed into her comfy lounge pants, but as comfy as they were, they did nothing to make her feel better. Something was going to be terribly wrong in Wander Creek if Carmen and Mona didn't get a hold of themselves. And something told Abby, that until they did, she would remain in the middle, with Mona and Carmen at opposite battle stations, and Abby stranded in the battlefield between them.

CHAPTER 3

*A*bby awoke in her dark apartment, the sun another two hours from rising. Another typical cold and dark morning in northern Minnesota. *Seems like winter nights are even longer here than they were in Minneapolis.* As she made herself the first cup of coffee of the morning, she observed that the gloomy darkness mirrored her mood. She walked around her small apartment turning on lamps and clicked the gas fireplace on. The aroma of the coffee, combined with the cozy glow of the lamplight and the warmth of the gas flames began to soothe her. Whatever was going on between Mona and Carmen had to be between them. Abby couldn't get involved. She owned two businesses, had just hired a new manager for the Book Box, and Black Friday was three weeks away. She didn't have time to play referee. She couldn't, and wouldn't, take sides. Abby would have to rise above all that. *I will be the adult in the room.* Abby hoped that Carmen would decide to do the same.

Abby dressed in her typical work clothes: dressy jeans, a silk blouse and blazer set, and cream-colored wedge-heeled boots that matched her top and pinched her toes to no end. After a minor application of make-up, she bounced down the stairs. It was still early, not yet seven, but she and Carmen were meeting at the Book Box at seven, and Carmen was a stickler for punctuality.

Abby turned on the lights to make her way through the store, then turned them off again when she reached and unlocked the front door. Just as she plunged the sales floor into darkness, a shadow moved past the front store window, then she saw a lithe figure dart across Main Street, hit Wolf Path Lane, and disappear around the corner of Whisk kitchen store. Hand still on the door handle, Abby blinked, as if either trying to conjure the figure or shake it away. Had she really seen that? She put the thought away to return to later. She could not be late. Afterall, what was she going to do, chase after a shadow in the frigid early morning darkness? Instead, she stepped out into the crisp winter air and hurried next door to the Book Box.

Before Abby could even reach for the door handle, Carmen opened the door and Abby entered, instantly surrounded by the scent of vanilla and hazelnut.

"Here," Carmen said, handing Abby her second steaming cup of the morning. "Hazelnut cappuccino with a dash of vanilla."

Abby took a sip. "How on earth did you make this here?" she asked.

Carmen pointed to a small area where she had set up a beverage station. "I brought my fancy espresso machine from the Paperie," she said. "In fact, I brought a lot of things I thought would translate well into a bookstore." She took a few steps into the store, Abby following, sipping her delicious drink.

"Remember these armchairs?" she asked, and Abby nodded. "I used these as client chairs at the Paperie, but now they're great for customers to plunk down and do some reading. Then, of course, buy the book," she added.

"But how did you … ?" Abby wondered out loud how on earth Carmen fit two armchairs in her Mini.

"Oh, I had them delivered. Along with a bunch of other stuff. A guy owed me a favor. No big deal."

Carmen continued, pointing to another corner. "I've added a display of greeting cards, using my remaining stock from when I sold my store. I hope you don't mind. I curated them and only have greeting cards with a reading or bookish theme."

Abby was impressed with Carmen's initiative, but wasn't surprised. Her friend and mentor had run a successful small business for thirty years.

"This is wonderful, Carmen," Abby said. "You must have been up all night. The store is really coming together."

"I was up for a long time," Carmen admitted. "I had a lot on my mind and now I want to apologize to you for what happened at dinner last night. I worked through my emotions while working on the store. I had many hours to get this apology worded right before going to bed, so I did get a lot done in the meantime. But, anyway, I shouldn't have let Mona get under my skin last night. I should have just ignored her darts. I should have responded with kindness."

Abby squeezed her friend's arm. "Apology not necessary, but reluctantly accepted. Now show me what else you've done in the past twelve hours. I can't believe how close you are to being ready, and opening day is still two weeks away."

∾

The next evening after the stores closed, Abby invited Carmen and Jessica to look at the paintings in her apartment. Fresh eyes would bring fresh perspectives. And maybe shed some light on the mystery.

After the trio enjoyed their glasses of Merlot, Abby retrieved the paintings from her closet and placed them carefully on the dining table.

"These are what I wanted you guys to see," Abby said, as Carmen and Jessica stood on either side of her.

Abby quickly explained how she and Ken found the paintings and how much she wanted to learn who they belonged to, and how they wound up plastered into a wall in the Book Box.

"These really are quite lovely," Carmen said, bending over to inspect each painting closely. "Even though you can't really see the face, I'd say it's definitely the same man in each painting, don't you think? See the slope of the shoulders? And look at the ears. They're almost identical in each."

"Oh boy, another mystery man," Jessica joked. "Don't tell Mona. That's all we need, another intrigue." Jessica was referring to a mystery they previously helped Mona solve.

Abby rolled her eyes. "Well, it did work out pretty well the last time. Mona and Marcus are definitely going steady, or something like that." Abby tried not to think about the little velvet jewelry box. How relieved she would be if it turned out that Marcus planned to propose to Mona. That would put her mind at ease and settle the uncertainty for good.

She looked up as Jessica was saying, "Hello. Earth to Abby."

Both Carmen and Jessica looked at her quizzically.

"Sorry," Abby said to her friends. "I didn't mean to space out like that."

"You have been distracted quite a bit lately," Jessica observed. "Do you want to talk about it?"

Abby answered brightly, eager to change the subject. She did not want to tell them about Ken. Or the little jewelry box switcheroo she witnessed. "There's nothing to talk about. I guess I was just ruminating over these paintings." She gestured to the first one. "The man in the meadow is my favorite. I love the light blues in his shirt set against the vibrant red and golds of the leaves."

Carmen asked Jessica, "Do you recognize him? You've lived here for a pretty long time, right?"

Jessica squinted at one of the paintings, then at the other. "Nobody is coming to mind." She pulled her cell phone from her pants pocket and snapped a photo of each painting. "Maybe if I study them a bit more, something will hit me." She slid her phone back into her pocket. "But now I have to scram. I think my ex might start charging me for every minute I'm late picking up Aiden, just like the pre-school does."

Once Jessica was gone Carmen and Abby settled on the couch.

"In the thirty years I owned the Paperie in Minneapolis, nothing nearly as exciting as finding works of art in the wall ever happened there. Once, a homeless man came into the store around Christmastime and walked around bellowing out Christmas carols. It was actually kind of sweet because he did sort of look like Santa Claus. And he could really sing. Anyway, here we are at the Book Box, not even open yet, and bam, a cryptic set of paintings emerges from a wall as if by magic."

"I suppose they're only cryptic because we don't know the man. But someone knows him. If it's a real person. Did you notice there's no signature anywhere? That is surprising, don't you think?"

Carmen nodded. "These paintings have an intimate feel to them," she said thoughtfully. "I almost feel like we're interrupting these moments that were meant to be between just two people—the painter and the subject."

"Maybe that's why they were hidden away," Abby mused, more determined than ever to solve the mystery.

CHAPTER 4

hen Carmen called to tell Abby the window display was complete and she should visit once the shops closed, Abby made a bee line for the Book Box. She couldn't wait to see what Carmen had come up with. The butcher paper was still taped over the front window display, still blocking the view from passersby on Main Street.

"Ta, da," Carmen yelled as Abby stepped into the store, spreading her arms in a grand flourish.

"Oh, Carmen," Abby breathed. "This is spectacular!"

Carmen did a little bow. "Why thank you, madame. Why don't you take a closer look and I'll get us a glass of wine from upstairs."

Abby moved closer and stood where she had the full view of the display, and gasped. It would be even more charming from the sidewalk looking in.

Somehow, Carmen had brought a small tree, about eight feet tall, an actual tree, into the store and secured it against one wall of the window display. It looked like she had made the crown of the tree out of wire forms of some sort and covered them with layer upon layer of the most realistic artificial leaves Abby had ever seen—scarlets, golds, and deep oranges—and intertwined everything with soft yellow fairy lights that gave the scene a charming and calming feel.

Leaning against the tree in a seated position was a mannequin of a man wearing a light blue shirt and khaki pants and sitting on green fake grass and a smattering of fall leaves. His mannequin hands, which looked almost real, held a book as if he were reading. Except for the positioning of the book. Abby knew who it was right away. The man in the meadow. Her eyes misted with tears, and she had to shake her head to restore her senses.

To complete the scene, Carmen had placed a small stack of books, a picnic basket, and a leather backpack on the ground.

Two professionally produced signs were attached by clear fishing line to the ceiling and hung directly over the display. One read, "Welcome to the Book Box." The next read, "Reading is great, anytime, anyplace."

~

Abby had no idea why she was so nervous. She had socialized with Mona and Marcus many times. Was she intimidated by their massive individual fortunes? Combined they probably possessed the equivalent of the gross national product of a small country. No, she decided. She wasn't intimidated by their wealth. After all, she had been a multi-millionaire once herself, and had mingled in the same circles at the top echelon of Minneapolis society. No, the issue was in fact the ongoing feud between Mona and Carmen. But maybe this dinner would help. If she could muster the courage, Abby planned to lay it all out on the table and find a solution once and for all.

Abby met Marcus and Mona at the front door, led them through the store and up the stairs to her apartment. When the couple entered, Mona kindly complimented Abby on the already set farmhouse table. "Why Abby, keep it up and I'm going to have to hire you at the Inn. This looks amazing."

Abby never tired of getting compliments from Mona, which were usually few and far between. "Why thank you, Mona. Coming from you, well, that means a lot. Why don't you two have a seat on the couch and I'll get your drinks. Mona, dry vodka martini okay? And Marcus, would you like an Old Fashioned?"

Marcus didn't answer her question. It was as if he hadn't heard her. Abby turned and saw Marcus' gaze laser focused on the two paintings leaning against the wall under the window that looked from her apartment down onto Main Street. He seemed startled and got up so quickly from his seat on the couch that he jolted the ottoman and jiggled the plates of appetizers. He didn't seem to notice as he walked hurriedly to the window. Then he seemed mesmerized.

"Where did you get these?" he asked, almost demanded, in a tone of voice Abby had never heard in him before.

Abby looked at Mona, whose head jerked up at the sound of his voice. She spilled a portion of her martini onto her lap.

Marcus was a deep thinker. Abby knew he was meticulous in his business dealings, which had certainly helped him to grow his family's multi-national media conglomerate into the behemoth it was today. That Marcus had an eye for detail was evident when he removed his cell phone from his pocket, opened the flashlight app and shone it slowly over the paintings.

By then, Abby and Mona had joined him, and Abby quickly explained how she and Ken had discovered the paintings in the wall of the Book Box during renovations. She explained Ken's wonderment at how they had wound up behind a plaster wall. Someone had gone to a great deal of effort to hide them. And whether they meant to or not, to preserve them.

31

"Do you have any idea who did these paintings?" Abby asked quietly. "Or who the subject is?"

Marcus turned off his flashlight and returned to his seat on the couch, visibly baffled, as if he had just found pieces of a puzzle that had been abandoned long ago.

"I never thought I'd see them again," he explained quietly.

Abby fidgeted with her bracelets, anxious for Marcus to hurry it along, but restrained from giving him a rolling motion with her hand, to indicate that he should speed it up. If Abby was going to discover the story behind the paintings, she'd have to let Marcus tell it his way, at his own pace.

"Forty years ago, Elise—that's my sister, as you know—met a bookseller in Paris at one of those kiosks along the Seine River. He was an American, and was only there for a few weeks, helping a friend, the kiosk owner, who was having surgery. But he was fluent in French, just like Elise, and was able to manage the kiosk and operate it with no trouble. Elise sold her original paintings not far from there. This American befriended her, and introduced her to the great French writers and intellectuals. They fell in love. She painted his portrait. Twice, obviously. At least twice, anyway. When she decided to leave Paris and return home to the states, he begged her to stay with him in Paris, or at least let him accompany her back to the States. She refused. The night before she left, she gave him those paintings."

"But how did the paintings get to Wander Creek?" Abby asked, mesmerized by the story of Marcus' eccentric sister who had decided she was not going to let anything like love get in the way of her plan to dedicate her life to art.

"I first saw them in Elise's apartment in Paris, years ago, when she was finishing them," Marcus said. She said she was going to give them to the bookseller. I think it was a consolation prize for her leaving him. The love of her life. The love of his life."

"I still don't understand," Abby said, now visibly impatient.

"You will," Marcus said, "just hold on."

"Two years after Elise returned to Wander Creek, a man named Dennis Grey opened a bookstore next to the building that housed Elises' art gallery, which now houses your Paper Box."

Mona had been uncharacteristically quiet during the exchange between Abby and Marcus, but now she gasped. "But that's Dennis—our Dennis—the one I've known for years. So he followed Elise to Wander Creek." Mona clapped her hands in delight, proud that she had figured out the mystery. "And he brought the paintings with him. How romantic. He owned that bookshop for decades before he sold it to Abby."

"For a time, it was romantic," Marcus said, continuing his story. "I think Elise was flattered that Dennis went to so much trouble just to be close to her, and for a time they rekindled their love affair."

"Well," Abby prompted. "What happened?"

"It's hard to tell," Marcus said. "Elise is such a private person and being the odd duck that she is, well, that makes it doubly difficult to understand what happened. They were together for two years. The Christmas of the second year, Dennis snuck onto her property and decorated her gazebo to the nines. He blindfolded her and escorted her through the meadow to her gazebo, then the story goes he went down on one knee and proposed. When she rejected him, he retreated to his store. And as far as I can tell, he remained in Wander Creek so he would be around in case Elise changed her mind."

"But she didn't," Abby said, picking up the story. "Instead, she closed down her art gallery and became a hermit, coming to town only on the rarest of occasions."

"Exactly," Marcus agreed. "And not long after Elise rejected his proposal, she changed her last name from Fairchild to Winters. No one knows why. It seems so random, but knowing my sister she was most likely trying to make some kind of statement. Maybe it's a reference to the season when Dennis proposed. I doubt we will ever know."

"How do you know all this?" Abby asked Marcus, feeling fairly certain that Elise would not have shared such personal information, even with her brother.

"Dennis told me," Marcus said. "Before he proposed he drove down to Minneapolis where I was living at the time and asked my permission to marry her. Our father had passed, so I guess he thought I was the next best thing. And when she rejected him, I think I was the first person he called."

"Oh, that just breaks my heart," Abby said, remembering with special fondness the kind and gentle man who owned his bookstore until it became too difficult to be on his feet all day.

"But how did the paintings end up in the wall of Dennis's shop?" Mona asked. "That seems very dramatic."

"The whole story is dramatic," Abby pointed out. "What's another little flare?"

"The more important question," Mona interjected, "is where Dennis is now?"

Abby thought back to the conversations she'd had with him when they completed the sales documents. What had he said? She'd have to consult the sales papers and transfer of deed for Dennis' current address. Full of ideas for her new endeavor, Abby hadn't paid the least amount of attention to Dennis' plans.

Should she see if she could find Dennis? Wouldn't it be great to reunite him with Elise? *Now that seems pretty dramatic.* She was dying to know exactly why Dennis had gone to the trouble to hide those paintings. She knew it sounded crazy, but maybe if she got them back together, she would find the answer.

She lost all interest in helping Mona and Carmen mend their fences. That would have to wait. For now, at least.

$\sim$

"*L*ooks like someone is finally going to open a shop in the building between Whisk and the pharmacy," Abby was saying to Carmen over the phone during their semi-regular evening phone call. Whisk was the highly successful kitchen gadget specialty store caddy corner across the street from the Paper Box. The store between it and the pharmacy had been empty for a while.

"They've been working in there for a couple weeks now," Carmen said. "I've been keeping an eye on them. I'll be glad when they take that ugly tarp down. We can't even see the name of the store and it's such an eyesore."

"Yeah, me too," Abby said distractedly. "There has been a whole slew of workers going in and out and there are huge deliveries practically every day. I've seen constructions workers, plumbers, electricians, painters, and more. Whoever is over there, they seem like they are in a huge hurry to get the business up and running. It must be costing a fortune at the accelerated pace everyone is working. I'm sure they're paying tons of overtime."

"Can you tell what kind of business it's going to be?" Carmen asked.

"I haven't been able to tell," Abby said. "The deliveries have been coming in unmarked trucks. Like rental trucks."

"Maybe they're doing that on purpose, like it's something nefarious," Carmen suggested jokingly, but Abby took her seriously.

"Now why would they be in such a hurry? And why the unmarked trucks?" Abby wondered, feeling a finger of unease nudging her. "Something doesn't feel right."

"Why would you think that?" Carmen asked.

"Just a strange feeling I have," Abby said, rubbing her hands over her upper arms. "For some reason whenever I look over there it makes my skin crawl. Like there's something bad going on."

"That's a pretty huge leap, don't you think?" Carmen said.

"Did I ever tell you about the day my grandmother died?" asked Abby, not waiting for an answer. "The night before her death I had a dream about her. I was sleeping alone in my bed back at the lake house where I lived with Jake. He was out of town on business. Anyway, I dreamed that I woke up and sat up in bed and she was sitting there in her favorite chair, right there in my bedroom. She was wearing her favorite black-and-white checked suit, and smiling at me. Eventually I woke up for real. But I had this terrible feeling that something was wrong. I learned the next morning that my grandmother died in her sleep the previous evening."

"Wow," Carmen responded, obviously affected. "That's quite a dream. Almost like a premonition."

"Yeah, it was pretty freaky. But the feeling I have now about that building is similar to the feeling I had when my grandmother died, like something very bad is about to happen," Abby offered.

"I sincerely hope you're wrong," Carmen said, "what with having just opened the Book Box and all."

There was a brief silence on the line, until Abby continued, "And on top of this new business, I feel like someone is buying up land and property in the area," Abby said. "Just a few things that Mona has said."

"Like what?" Carmen asked.

"In addition to the shady building across the way there's another business building on the outskirts of town that recently sold. It's been on the market for so long that there isn't even a sign out front. It's like the owner just gave up. I think its most recent iteration was warehouse space."

"What did it used to be before it was a warehouse?" Carmen asked.

"The story is it wasn't originally built as a warehouse, but nobody seems to know exactly what it used to be," Abby responded. "People have talked about buying it for various uses—self storage, art studios, wedding venues—but nothing has come to pass. Until now."

"Let's go take a look," Carmen said.

"What? Now?" Abby asked, glancing at the time on her cell phone.

"Why not?" Carmen said. "It's late on a Monday evening and no one will be around. Maybe we can find a way in. If it's been vacant as long as you say it has, then there are bound to be some broken windows we can crawl through so we can look around. Meet me out back at the Mini in five."

"That is if we don't slash an artery climbing past the jagged glass," Abby muttered, knowing full well that she would go along with Carmen. That she really wanted to go. She needed to figure out what was going on in Wander Creek. This made her think of the lithe figure darting around in the dark. Grabbing her coat, Abby let herself out the back door into the alley and headed toward Carmen's Mini.

"Want me to drive?" Abby asked.

"Now that I think about it, I think we'd be much more discreet if we walked," said Carmen. "This is a small town. Either of our cars parked in front of the warehouse would be noticed instantly. How far do you think it is from here?"

"Maybe a mile, mile and a half?"

"Nice night for a stroll," said Carmen.

Abby instantly knew that Carmen was right—her Bronco and Carmen's yellow Mini would stick out like a sore thumb.

The pair walked stealthily down Main Street, all the storefronts closed for business and plunged into darkness. They took a left on Maple Lane and when they hit Hickory Street walked several more blocks.

"There it is," Abby whispered, though there was obviously no one around to overhear her.

"Why are we whispering?" Carmen whispered back.

"I don't know," Abby said, continuing to whisper. "It just feels like the right thing to do under the circumstances. Come on, let's get off the street and see if there's a way in on the back side of the building."

Moonlight bathed the warehouse, which was an unremarkable but very large three-story red brick building. It had a pair of large wooden doors as the front entrance, with rows of ten large and tall arched windows protected with iron grating on either side of the entrance. Some of the windows had broken panes, probably having falling victim to the mischievousness of local teenage boys. There was a steeply pitched roof with a cupola. The building was rectangular, the ends being long enough to accommodate six each of the arched windows. In the center of the back side there was a single loading dock with a large rollup door, with another pair of wooden personnel doors just off to the side of that. The building did not appear to be dilapidated, but it clearly needed some TLC.

With the welcome assistance of the moonlight, Carmen and Abby felt their way around to the back of the building. Carmen reached into an inside coat pocket and came out with a long black flashlight, which she clicked on and trained on the back of the building.

"What are you doing?" Abby hissed. "What if someone sees us?"

Carmen clicked off the flashlight. "I just wanted to get my bearings. Take a few steps to the right and a few steps forward and there's a smaller door. It looks like it's hanging by one hinge. Hopefully it's not locked."

The two crept forward, Carmen leading the way, Abby close behind, her hand resting on Carmen's shoulder. Carmen pushed the door open a bit, and the one hinge preventing the door from crashing to the ground gave such a screech that the women jumped. They waited a minute, but no one responded to the sound.

"We need to do this bandaid style," Abby suggested. "Just shove the door open the whole way and get it over with in one smooth motion."

Carmen did as Abby suggested, and the door screeched again, and suddenly the two were standing inside the building. They waited, but there was no sound or any indication that someone had heard the noise.

"What now?" Carmen asked.

"I have no idea," Abby hissed. "This was your hair-brained idea. I have no idea what to do."

"Sure, you do," Carmen said. "Just use your imagination. You had no idea how to open a business, but you did it anyway."

"I think I'll let you do the imagining," Abby said. "I'm just here for moral support."

"We'll just look around for a minute, then we'll get the heck out of here," Carmen instructed.

Carmen shined her flashlight around the massive warehouse. It was obvious that it had been used for storage, just as Abby had said. But, to Abby's utter surprise, it was, in a word, beautiful.

"Look at those exposed beams! They're huge!" Abby said, as Carmen shone her light on the ceiling perhaps thirty feet above their heads. "They are gorgeous."

Carmen shone her flashlight slowly around to illuminate the walls, walking over to get a closer look. "Just look at this wood. It's solid." She clanked the knuckle of her middle finger against the planking, which made a solid, satisfying sound. "All it needs is a good washing and some new stain." She then pointed the beam to the floor and scrubbed her foot back and forth to sweep away the dust, revealing wide tongue and groove planks, scratched up a bit, but appropriately dented and distressed. "This floor looks old. I wonder when this place was built?" she said. "If someone cleaned this place up a little, I bet it could be a real showplace.

Look, there's even a small, elevated area, like a stage, right there in the middle."

"Hmmm," Abby mused, imagining—as Carmen had suggested—what it might look like after renovations. She saw in her mind's eye fairy lights wrapped around the ceiling beams and bunting and arrangements of flowers surrounding the stage area. "I bet someone is going to turn this into a wedding venue, or for parties, special events, things like that," she speculated.

The pair walked deeper into the space. "It certainly is big enough for that, and for smaller parties you could bring in rolling partitions to divide it up. What's that over there, in that back corner?" Carmen asked, pointing with her finger.

The two moved toward the back corner, stepping carefully, and came to a series of rooms separated from the main space. There were doors marked MEN and WOMEN, and one marked KITCHEN. Abby turned on her cell phone flashlight and dragged Carmen by the elbow into the ladies' room. She reached out and turned on the faucet on one of the two sinks, which caused an immediate knocking and hissing sound.

"What?" Abby asked with a shrug of her shoulders. "I was just curious to see if the new owner turned on the utilities or not."

Carmen rolled her eyes, even though it was too dark for Abby to notice. "Just be careful is all I'm saying. I don't want to be arrested for trespassing."

"I have a few friends in the police department," Abby assured her friend. "It might not keep us from being arrested but they can probably keep us from spending the night in jail."

"Hardy, har," Carmen said sarcastically. "You are so hilarious. Now let's get out of here. I don't want to press our luck."

Carmen trained her light on the door through which they had entered, and they walked carefully toward it. But on the way Abby made Carmen stop and shine her flashlight slowly around the whole place, just so she could get one more look.

Why do I have such a bad feeling about this place?

CHAPTER 5

*N*ow that there was a mystery business set to open across the street from Abby's store, and some mystery person was buying up other property, Abby's bad feelings continued. She didn't know why, but she knew that things would soon fall into place in all the wrong ways.

Abby and Jessica were at their usual table at the Bistro, waiting for Mona to join them for a drink. When Mona swept in wearing a beautiful light blue thigh length winter coat with white faux fur collar, complimented by a snow-white faux fox fur roller hat, of course all heads turned. The patrons who did not stare at least glanced as she removed her coat and hung it on the rack at the front entrance, revealing a smart beige pantsuit. After all these years in Wander Creek, Mona still fascinated her fellow citizens.

After ordering a dry vodka martini, Mona got straight to the point with, "So what is it you need?"

"Why do you think we need something?" Abby asked innocently.

"Oh, please," Mona said. "You two have never initiated a little

Bistro soiree with me. It's always *me* who organizes all the outings and adventures and social gatherings for the three of us."

The waitress brought Mona's drink, and she practically moaned with pleasure as she picked up the frilly toothpick and delicately chomped the green olive, then lifted the glass to her lips and took a satisfying first sip. She returned the glass to the table.

"So, what is it that I can help the two of you with?"

Abby debriefed Mona on what she had learned about the warehouse, and what she speculated the new owners were going to do with it. She was careful not to mention the part about breaking and entering and trespassing, and even more careful not to mention Carmen's name.

"Do you know who bought it?" Abby asked. "Or who bought the building across from the Paper Box? I'm dying to know."

"Why don't you just walk across the street and ask?" Mona inquired.

"Abby has a funny feeling about what's going on," Jessica explained. "Like something isn't quite right."

Mona took another fortifying sip of her martini and sat it back down on the table before responding. "I wasn't sure if I should tell you this, but given that you're so curious about all the property being snatched up, and that you are a significant business leader in the community, I think I should tell you."

"That sounds ominous," Abby said, exchanging a glance with Jessica.

"For you it probably is," Mona agreed. "A few days ago, while I was at McDonald's in Two Harbors, I ran into Naomi."

Abby interrupted, almost shocked, equally with the Naomi part and the McDonalds part of Mona's revelation.

"What in the world were you doing at McDonalds?" Abby asked her elegant, sophisticated friend.

"What?" Mona quipped. "I like an Oreo McFlurry every now and then as much as anybody. Now stop interrupting me.

Naomi saw me, too, so of course I couldn't pretend I hadn't seen her."

"Sure, you could," Abby pouted. "I would have."

"Yes, but I don't have quite the contentious relationship with her that you had. And obviously still have."

Abby let her mind drift back to Naomi Dale's instant dislike, or more accurately, instant hatred of her when she first moved to Wander Creek. Through a series of coincidences and misunderstandings, Naomi actually believed that Abby had stolen not only her building, but also her boyfriend, and a valued employee.

Mona continued. "Anyway, Naomi was meeting with her lawyer to sign papers finalizing the sale of that big pole barn fiasco on the other side of the creek. She happened to mention, very coyly, I might add, that she also bought the warehouse that I heard you and Carmen decided to take a midnight walk to."

"Wait a second," Abby said, her blood pressure rising. "Back up to the part where you said Naomi is buying up property in Wander Creek. How on earth can she afford this? I know she didn't get much for selling the Beanery because the business wasn't in that great shape to begin with."

"You are not going to believe this," Mona gushed. "She won a state lottery while visiting friends in Virginia. She's rich. Not rich like me, of course, but rich enough to buy property and pretty much do whatever she wants."

"Where is she living?" Abby wanted to know. "Naomi used to live in the apartment above the coffee shop."

Mona didn't say anything, but instead looked down into her glass as if it held the wisdom of the ages.

"No," Abby guessed, "you didn't. Tell me you didn't."

"Darling, it's just business. You know I never turn away paying guests. In any event, she's only staying at the Inn for a few weeks until construction is completed on her new house out in North Pines."

North Pines was a posh new development about halfway

between Wander Creek and Two Harbors. It was gated, exclusive, and Abby was instantly and insanely jealous.

"So, who bought the building across the street from me?" Abby asked. "If it's Naomi, I will absolutely lose my mind."

"All I can tell you with confidence," Mona began, flicking her wrist and fluttering her red tipped fingers, "is that it's a corporation out of Delaware called IHAB, Inc. Looks like it's a shell corporation, and it's owned by another shell corporation in Delaware called IWGY, Ltd. But I'm pretty sure it's Naomi."

"How do you know all this?" Abby asked.

"I just asked around at the last planning commission meeting. It's not a secret, you know. It's all public information. But you have to know where and how to look, and who to talk to. But you'd have to look really deep and far to find the name of the person behind the shell companies."

"What kind of business names are IHAB and IWGY anyway?" Abby asked. "They sound so stupid."

"Probably stands for the initials of the owners, or family members, or something like that. Sometimes companies make up their names from nothing," Mona said.

"Like **Häagen-Dazs**," Jessica contributed.

In her confusion about what the heck Naomi was up to Abby had forgotten that Jessica was sitting right next to her.

"**Häagen-Dazs** doesn't mean anything," Jessica continued. "It's totally made up. And the owners put the two little dots above the first letter A to draw the customer's eye. Because it was so unusual to see, in the United States at least."

Abby didn't respond. "Where has Naomi been all this time since she left Wander Creek?" she asked Mona.

"She was in Virginia visiting an old college friend," Mona said.

"I can't imagine that Naomi has any friends," Abby quipped.

"Well, apparently, more like obviously, she does," Mona continued. "She left Virginia and went on a world cruise. She was supposed to be gone for nine months but after staying at an ice hotel in Sweden, she decided she wanted to open one in Minnesota, so she came back."

"You've got to be kidding me," Abby laughed. "What does she plan to do when the ice melts? She'll have to start all over again the next winter."

"That's probably why she's buying property. After seeing the flaws in her ice hotel idea."

"Same old Naomi," Abby said. "Stirring up craziness wherever she goes."

"You didn't hear this from me," Mona whispered, looking around to make sure the other customers weren't listening, "And of course, I would never, ever, speak ill of or gossip about my guests."

"Of course not," Abby and Jessica said in unison.

"Now that we have that straight, do spill," Abby commanded Mona.

"Well, Naomi told me about this idea she had about opening a B&B where the guests pretend to be in jail and the owners pretend to be their jailers. The imprisoned would be served their meals behind bars, and some guests could pay extra to be put in solitary confinement. Things like that. And both the prisoners and jailers would be in costume. She was going to charge two-thousand dollars a night."

"And what happened to that idea?" Abby asked.

"I talked her out of it," Mona admitted.

"Afraid of the competition?" Abby quipped.

"Don't be silly. There is no competition for the Wander Inn, except for the boutique hotel *I'm* building."

"I would love to see her open a jail hotel and fall flat on her face," Abby said. "Maybe you can talk her back into it."

"Rather harsh, don't you think, my dear?" Mona chastised Abby before changing the subject.

Abby really could not believe Mona was actually trying to defend Naomi.

There wasn't much to say after that. The women finished their drinks, and chit chatted about inconsequential things. Why was Mona defending Naomi? And why was she being so mean to Carmen?

That evening, safe in her cozy apartment, Abby changed into her comfy pajamas and settled under a blanket on the couch in front of the gas fireplace. The ever-present conundrum with her two friends was really making her feel terrible.

She thought to herself, *the common denominator in the tension between Mona and Carmen is me. Am I doing something wrong? And if I am, how do I figure out what, and how do I stop?*

And, she didn't want to admit it, but she knew it was no coincidence that Naomi had returned at the very same time a shell corporation—two shell corporations—had bought the empty storefront across the street from her, and probably the warehouse, and who knows what other businesses around Wander Creek. And, whoever was doing all that work on the building across the street—it seemed more and more that it had to be Naomi—was keeping everything a secret. Naomi must be laying low at the Wander Inn. Surely she would have guessed that Mona would reveal to Abby that her nemesis was back in town. And maybe that was Naomi's plan after all, to stealthily make Abby squirm, first with the renovations of the secretive business across the street, and then by making sure Abby knew she was in Wander Creek, but also making sure Abby never saw her. Except —could that have been Naomi slipping in and out of the shadows that morning?

I have a really, really, really bad feeling about this, she told the flickering gas logs.

CHAPTER 6

*W*hen Thanksgiving Day finally arrived, Abby was relieved to have a day off. She was looking forward to spending time with Ken, too, confident in the thought that he would never propose to her in a public setting.

Like Mona's famous annual Christmas feast, her Thanksgiving spread was not to be missed either. If one was lucky enough to be invited, one went. And in Wander Creek, one did not say no to Mona. But before she had even been invited, Carmen had declared that she would be at the Book Box all day Thanksgiving Day making sure everything was perfect for the Black Friday grand opening, even if it took all night. Carmen apparently had no problem whatsoever saying no to Mona.

This year's Thanksgiving meal was served in the large dining room. The grand dining table occupied the center of the room and was elegantly set with the Inn's finest china and silver impeccably arranged on a silky white taffeta tablecloth. The crystal water glasses had all been topped off, and the champagne flutes beckoned to be filled with any of the fine selection of sparkling wines chilling in silver ice buckets on the buffet table.

The festivities were to begin promptly at noon. Telly and the temporary sous chef Mona had hired for the holiday season had just placed the steaming silver serving trays on the buffet table, which seemed to stretch forever down the dining room wall. Abby never liked to be the first one at any social event, but somehow, she often found herself the first one to arrive. This Thanksgiving dinner was no different.

"Hi, Abby," Telly said over his shoulder when he noticed Abby enter the dining room. "Mona's helping in the kitchen. She'll be right out." He continued his work and was about to head back into the kitchen when he suddenly turned to Abby and asked, "Carmen doing okay? I understand she won't be joining us today."

"I tried to convince her to come, but she's a bit stubborn. She's so focused on tomorrow's grand opening. There was just no convincing her," Abby explained. She then added, "But yes, she's doing great. I'll tell her you asked."

Abby slowly walked around the table, admiring the elegance and grandeur of the room. Her eyes had just settled on the place cards at the head of the table all lined up in a row when Mona made her entrance. "Well, hello dear," she said pleasantly to Abby.

"I noticed you haven't arranged the place cards yet. Want me to do it?" Abby offered, thinking it would be fun to arrange the seating for this year's guests.

"Not necessary, dear," Mona said. "I've decided to throw caution to the wind this year and let people sit wherever they choose."

Abby picked up a couple of place cards bearing names that she did not recognize. "David? Melinda?" she asked with a puzzled look on her face.

"Guests of the Inn, my dear, remember? Renting out rooms is how I make such a comfortable living. They get hungry, too," Mona reminded Abby, turning her back as she fussed with one of the gorgeous floral arrangements on the buffet table.

"Oh, of course," Abby said just as some of her fellow guests began to enter the dining room. Abby found herself standing and small talking with a growing group of people, to include overnight guests David and Melinda and six others, and Jessica, then Ken, and then Marcus.

Mona joined the group and welcomed everyone to the Inn, and then explained the place card situation. "Just take your place card and choose any empty chair you'd like," she instructed.

Within a few minutes, everyone who was supposed to be there had arrived, picked up their place card, and chosen a seat. The eight guests from the Inn stayed in a group, sitting opposite each other, two couples on one side and two on the other in the chairs closest to the head of the table. No one had dared, of course, to choose the head of the table. Everyone knew that belonged to Mona. Abby was impressed that Jessica had chosen the foot of the table, directly opposite Mona. Marcus was next to Jessica and opposite Abby, and the chair opposite Ken sat empty, even though it had been set for a diner.

Carmen could have sat there, Abby thought, and hated herself when another thought popped into her head, that she was glad Carmen *wasn't* there.

Mona was the last person to take her seat, but as she approached the head of the table Marcus quickly arose, hurried to the head of the table, and pulled out her chair. Obviously delighted, Mona sat. "Thank you, dear," she said, patting Marcus' hand, which rested for more than a moment on Mona's shoulder.

Mona then went around the table and had each person hold up their place card as a way of introduction. Each person was supposed to say just their first name, where they were from, whether they had been to Wander Creek before, and if they chose, what they did for a living. It turned out to be a fun icebreaker.

Soon the entire group was lined up at the buffet table, filling their plates with Telly's masterpieces.

Telly had outdone himself, with a beautiful herb-glazed turkey, a grilled vegetable medley of sweet potatoes and carrots, garlic mashed potatoes, a beet and arugula salad, chestnut and fennel stuffing, a green bean asparagus casserole, balsamic roasted red onions, gravy galore, fresh yeast rolls and three types of cranberry sauce.

Many made multiple trips to the buffet, encouraged on by both Mona and Telly.

The meal was festive and delicious, as it was every year. There was laughter, happy conversations, goodwill galore, flowing champagne—who could ask for more? Abby loved coming to the Inn for these events. Everyone was on their best behavior, everyone wore their best outfits, everyone seemed happy and hopeful.

As the diners made their way to the parlor for dessert, Abby stood off to the side letting Marcus and Ken finish a conversation as they walked. As she waited, Telly stepped up close and said, "Will you please wish Carmen good luck for tomorrow? In case I don't make it over to tell her myself?"

"Sure," Abby said, so pleased by Telly's interest.

Then Telly added, "From me. Good luck from me."

Later, over pie and cider in the parlor, Abby sought Marcus out and plopped down beside him on the couch, determined to find out if he planned to propose to Mona. If he said yes, then she could be almost certain that the ring in the black velvet box belonged to him and not Ken. And what she happened to catch a

A PLACE FOR CHRISTMAS

glimpse of was Marcus showing Ken the ring, and not the other way around.

"What a feast," Abby said, blowing out her breath. "I think I may have to roll home. Mona sure knows how to throw a party. Any man would be lucky to have her."

Marcus gave Abby a sideways glance.

Oops, I may have over done it, Abby thought, scolding herself.

"Not that I mean that you are the man that would be lucky to have her," Abby continued, digging herself further into a hole. "What I mean to say is that you already have her. I mean, if you wanted to have her."

Marcus held up his hand. "Why don't I put you out of your misery," he suggested, laughing.

"Please do," Abby said, laughing along with him. "I don't know what got into me."

"I do," he said, his eyes twinkling.

"What do you mean," Abby asked, more confused than ever.

"I mean, you're curious to know what I'm up to because you saw something. Or think you saw something."

Abby stared at his rugged, handsome face for a long time, cocking her head as if he might be more inclined to offer an explanation if she looked at him sideways. She didn't know what to say next, so an awkward silence hung between them until Marcus finally broke it.

"You want to know what my intensions are with Mona because you caught me on my phone that one time looking at engagement rings on the internet. Or at least you thought you did. Remember? But that was a very old search. I was just closing my browser windows. Mona is always on me about that. I think sometimes I have five hundred open at one time."

"You don't say," Abby said distractedly, knowing for sure that she had no recollection whatsoever of catching Marcus looking at engagement rings, or anything, for that matter, on his cell phone. *Wonder why he thinks I saw his cell phone?* Was he telling the truth, or maybe playing with her? If the internet search was old, as he claimed, then the little black box could belong to either Marcus or Ken. But if Marcus wasn't being forthcoming about his internet search, then the ring box belonged to Ken. It would have to. There was no other logical explanation. Or was there? *This is driving me crazy. I'm tying myself into knots trying to figure this out.*

"I'm pretty sure your intentions with Mona are nothing but honorable," Abby said, "otherwise I think we would have found you out by now."

"Very true," Marcus agreed, grinning widely. "And it's not like I'm after her money."

Mona arrived at the couch just then and Marcus rose and kissed her hand, and they floated off to chat with other guests.

Abby wanted to kick the coffee table and make the empty cider glasses shake. But she had a better idea and rose from the couch to seek out Ken. If she couldn't solve the mystery of the jewelry box, maybe she could solve another one.

~

"*W*ell, this is a first," Ken said when Abby approached him as he was finishing his pie. She suggested a walk to burn off the Thanksgiving Day calories. "Usually I'm the one who suggests the outdoor activities," he said, laughing playfully.

"Yes, but I always go along with whatever you suggest, am I right?"

"I think there might have been one time when I suggested we go ice fishing, and I seem to remember you backing away from me, a look of horror on your face, before you took off running down Main Street," he said, smiling widely.

Ken was joking, of course, but there was a nugget of truth

here. He was simply teasing her about her first, and last, experience with ice fishing. Actually, it was really her first and last time that she had walked on a frozen lake. And not just walked on it, but walked far out onto the ice, way across to the middle where the ice fishermen were doing their thing. It had not gone well, ending in a panic attack, and now an abiding fear of standing on frozen bodies of water.

Hand-in-hand, Abby and Ken sought out Mona to thank her for her hospitality and take their leave. When they arrived at the Paper Box, Abby quickly jogged up the stairs to her apartment and donned some warmer clothes and slipped on her favorite pair of hiking boots. It had snowed several inches over the last few days, so she picked the pair with the best tread. A few moments later, she reappeared at the foot of the stairs, and then walked over to Ken.

"Where to, my dear?" Ken asked, holding the front door open with his elbow while adjusting the straps on his dark red plaid mad bomber cap with faux sheepskin lining.

Only Ken could pull off such a mad-cap style, and make it look totally normal, Abby thought.

"I was thinking we'd take the bridge across the creek, then follow the path," Abby said. "And maybe walk to the second overlook, that is if I can still feel my fingers and we haven't been flattened by snowmobilers or bowled over by cross-country skiers."

"You make it sound so appealing," Ken said as they strolled down Main Street, and then turned left on Wolf Path Lane, which, as far as Abby knew, did not attract wolves. "How can I resist a treacherous walk that I may not survive?"

Abby punched his arm, then took his mittened hand. She loved this man so much. When she saw his face as he entered her store or heard his tread on the stairs leading up to her apartment, her heart summersaulted and her stomach tingled. There was no question that she wanted to be by his side, and not with anyone else. But was she ready for a second marriage after the first ended in such a disaster? Literally.

Ken was her first friend in Wander Creek. Their friendship developed quickly, then they fell in love despite a few bumps along the way.

Although he was as handsome as an actual Ken doll, Abby loved Ken for his sense of humor and his openness. Ken never said anything he didn't mean. He didn't take life too seriously but could buckle down and be as serious as anybody when the occasion called for it.

As they stepped out onto the low hung but sturdily built bridge that stretched northward from the shoreline across the creek, Abby heard the whine of the snowmobiles in the distance as the outdoor adventurers bounced and maneuvered down the trail, revving their engines into a loud but familiar whirl of sound.

"That's something we've never done—snowmobiling," Ken said, following Abby as she stepped off the other end of the bridge and turned left off of the road and onto the trail leading into the forest.

Abby was surprised at herself, first trespassing with Carmen at that old warehouse, and now leading Ken, without his knowledge, on an excursion to trespass yet again. But honestly, was it really trespassing if she knew the person who owned the land? If Elise happened to see them, Abby could simply say they were out for a walk and wanted to say hello. Elise wouldn't believe it, of course, but maybe that excuse would keep her and Ken from going to jail. Plus, Abby felt that Marcus would be on her and Ken's side if Elise made a big stink.

"We're not just out for a stroll, are we?" Ken asked, coming to an abrupt halt. "I mean, don't get me wrong, I'm loving every minute with you out here in nature, but I have a feeling there's something more going on."

"Okay, busted. Marcus told me a strange story the other

evening and I can't stop thinking about it," Abby admitted. "I have a hunch about something, but I want to see it for myself."

"See what?"

"Marcus told me a story about Elise and the gazebo on her property. My hunch is that if she even decorates for Christmas, the only thing she does decorate is the gazebo."

"Come to think of it, I guess I've noticed that too, but only in the way of now that you mention it, I can't remember ever noticing any Christmas decorations on her cabin. I guess I never paid any attention to the gazebo. It's pretty far up from the creek and sort of hidden behind the trees. And besides, I've only stepped foot on Elise's place a handful of times. And each of those times I was invited."

"How far up from the creek?" Abby asked, turning her head so a sliver of the slate roof of Elise's rustic red clapboard cabin became visible through the thick evergreens. She also noticed the afternoon sun was making rapidly toward the horizon. *I bet it's pitch black in these woods when the sun goes down.*

"Please tell me you're not thinking what I think you're thinking," Ken said, blowing air out of his mouth which produced visible puffs of swirling vapor. Abby remembered when she was just beginning her life so far north and had quickly learned what it felt like to have your earlobes go numb as soon as you stepped outside.

"Okay, I won't tell you," Abby said, smiling slyly. "You probably think that I want to trespass in order to see the gazebo. But actually, I want to pay a call on Elise, but we will obviously get turned around on our way to the house and happen to wander by the gazebo first until I find my way. I mean, we find our way."

Ken groaned. "You've been spending too much time around Mona."

No doubt, Mona, who was larger than life, was a pretty big influence on Abby, for better or worse.

"Let's look at it this way," Abby said, leaving the trail and starting up the incline toward the border of Elise's property, which was clearly marked by a gigantic 'No Trespassing' sign nailed to a fir tree. "It's an adventure. You love adventures. Isn't your business all about adventures?"

"Not the illegal kind," Ken quipped. "All of my adventuring is on the up and up and doesn't involve sneaking around on private property."

Abby continued to walk toward Elise's and glanced over her shoulder with a 'come on already' look on her face.

Ken left the trail tracing Abby's footprints. When he caught up to her, he said, "Okay, we'll go with the story that we've come to see Elise and got lost on her property. But if it gets out that I can't successfully navigate ten acres of woods right across the creek from where I've lived for ten years, well, I'm not sure what that might do to my reputation as a bad-ass adventure outfitter."

Abby grabbed his hand and gave it a squeeze and a tug. Ken squeezed back and they scrambled up the snowy berm and ducked right past another 'No Trespassing' sign.

Ken pulled a breathless Abby up the final stretch of the incline —she really did need to work out more—and they emerged in a small clearing. Their eyes were immediately graced with a view of a small and attractive red gazebo, decked out like, well, like a Christmas tree at Christmas.

Ken whistled. "I guess your hunch was spot on. But how do you know this is the only thing she decorates?"

Abby was silent, just staring at the beautiful structure. Then she answered Ken's question.

"I don't," she said, and quickly brought Ken up to speed on what Marcus had told her about the paintings they found and the love affair between Dennis and Elise. "Maybe this is Elise's way of keeping a little bit of Dennis with her, just like the paintings somehow kept Elise close to Dennis. It's like something out of a Jane Austen novel."

Abby dropped Ken's hand and walked closer to the gazebo,

mesmerized. The snowfall from the previous night provided a delicate swaddling on the gazebo roof. The meadow—for some reason Abby found meadows to be more than a little romantic— was also covered in pristine snow, but footprints surrounded the gazebo. Someone had been here recently.

Ken noticed the footprints, too. "Maybe if Elise has already been here this morning checking on her decorations there's less of a chance that we'll run into her and have to tell her our ridiculous story."

But Abby wasn't really listening. She was just taking in the glorious vision before her. The gazebo was octagonal, and strands of white fairy lights made a fluttery curtain hanging down on all sides. Abby imagined what it would look like all lit up at night. Wide red ribbons wound around the stair rails and were tied off at the ends into big puffy bows. Boughs of fir, hemlock, and cedar, complete with plentiful blue berries, were strung along the railing that circled the gazebo.

"What is this?" Abby asked, reaching out with her gloved hand and touching a garland made of some sort of berried shrub.

"Not sure. Maybe winterberry?"

The large holly bushes framing the gazebo were also strung with red ribbons and white lights. Realistic looking fake red cardinals were delicately arranged within the leaves, as if at any moment they would take flight.

She heard Ken muttering behind her as he walked around the structure. "Looks like somebody ran electricity from the cabin down to the gazebo," he said, pointing to where the wire attached to the frame of the gazebo, although Abby wasn't looking. "Whoever did this sure did a great job with the electrical. It's all very professionally done, and there must be ten outlets."

"Hmmmm," Abby said, walking up onto the center of the gazebo, where she stopped in front of a Christmas tree, also beautifully decorated.

There were real wrapped presents under the tree. At least real

wrapped boxes. The ones Abby picked up all contained something heavy inside, probably so they wouldn't be carried off by
the wind. *Books?* Abby bent down to read the gift tags. She picked
up a smallish box, wishing she had her reading glasses with her.

"What the heck are you doing?" boomed an unfriendly voice.

Abby jumped, dropping the present, and put her hand to her
thumping chest.

"You scared me half to death," Abby said, adrenaline running
through her.

"I should hope so," the voice said forcefully, and a short, stout
woman appeared from behind the shrubs. She was dressed from
head-to-toe in dark blue outerwear. "There was a time when
landowners could execute trespassers without a trial, then be on
their merry way."

Abby was relieved when Ken said, "Now Elise, we didn't mean
any harm. We were walking along the path and saw the lights and
just came up to investigate."

"Right past the 'No Trespassing' signs, no doubt," the older
woman huffed, hands on hips. "And the lights aren't even on. No
way you could have seen them from the trail." She paused for
affect, then launched back into her tirade. "I might have expected
this from this, this, newcomer floozy," she said, gesturing toward
Abby, who was now cowering by the Christmas tree in the
gazebo, wishing she could disappear. "But from you, Ken Turner,
who have been a respected businessman in Wander Creek for a
decade? Well, you should know better. No doubt this interloper
made some kissy noises and you did whatever she asked."

"Now just a minute," Abby interjected hotly. "I resent that
statement. You may not remember, but you and I met last
Christmas at Mona's holiday meal. We sat next to each other.
And we had a very nice time."

"What do you think I am, stupid?" Elise Winters huffed. "Of
course I remember you. You're Abby Barrett and you opened a
stationery store in the building where I once had my gallery."

"That's right," Abby said, trying to distract Elise from the fact that they were still trespassing. At least the old woman hadn't brought a shot gun with her. Unless it was hidden under her long wool coat. "It's next to the old Pages book shop."

"I know what was next to my art gallery," Elise snapped.

"Sorry, of course," Abby apologized, "it's just that I was trying to tell you that I bought the store from Dennis and it's now the Book Box."

"Why would I care about that?" Elise asked. "Now you two be on your way. I don't ever want to catch you here again."

With that, Elise Winters turned and walked up the path toward her cabin, just as quietly as she had arrived.

Abby let out her breath and Ken moved to her side.

"Thanks for not telling that stupid story about us wanting to visit her," Abby said. "Obviously, she would have recognized the lie right away."

"That's old Elise," Ken said walking up the gazebo steps and holding out his hand. "Come on, let's get out of here. We don't want to upset her any more than we already have, and you can tell me why this decorated gazebo is so important to you. Over hot chocolates. With Kahlua. And whipped cream."

Abby took his hand, and he pulled her into an embrace, kissing her softly on the lips. "I can't think of a cozier way to spend the afternoon."

Once back in Abby's apartment, having discarded their outwear and boots, Abby made hot chocolate the way her mother taught her, in a pan with milk, unsweetened coco powder and sugar to taste. She poured it into two mugs and topped the steaming liquid with whipped cream and cinnamon."

"You make the best hot chocolate," Ken said, accepting the cup. "Now that I think of it, Kahlua would probably ruin it."

"Yes, I do," Abby said. "Now, let me tell you about Elise and the gazebo." When she had finished her story, Ken was silent for a long time. Abby wasn't sure if he was going to laugh or cry. More likely, neither.

"You know what all this means, don't you?" Ken finally said.

"It means Elise still carries a torch for Dennis," Abby said.

"Not just that," Ken added. "If what Marcus told you is true, she has carried a torch for him for decades."

Abby couldn't think of anything more heartbreaking. And she wanted to do something about it. But tomorrow was a big day and she had to stay focused. Ken left shortly thereafter, promising her again for the umpteenth time that he would be at the Book Box grand opening. And he would be on time.

CHAPTER 7

*B*efore leaving the Paper Box the morning of the grand opening, Abby hurriedly restocked Christmas wrapping paper displays, placing the festive rolls in a large, pretty basket decorated with fresh holly and red ribbons. It was six in the morning, and Abby was super anxious, like a kindergartner on her first day of school. She then walked through the store, straightened inventory where it needed to be straightened, refreshed a stack of blank journals, and restocked the many eco-friendly gifts made from recycled paper, such as clutch purses made from old gum wrappers and earrings made from old magazines.

She had adjusted the Paper Box's hours and today she would not open until noon so she could be at the Book Box with Carmen, and she knew she would miss a lot of traffic, and therefore sales.

I really need to get some help around here, she grumbled to herself.

The advent of Thanksgiving week meant the summer/fall tourist season was officially over. But that also meant the winter tourist season had officially begun. Wander Creek would still be hopping with tourists as the fall and winter adventurers and their cohorts and wives arrived. The summer fishermen would be replaced by ice fishermen. Fall and winter meant hunters, snow-mobilers, cross county skiers, snowshoers, and even the occasional dog sledder.

Abby peeked out the window to see how much snow was falling and was surprised to see that the tarp had been removed from the windows and awnings of the mystery building across the street. Her gaze moved up from the windows to the large yellow awning with the words *Naomi's Stationery and Books* printed in beautiful cursive writing.

Abby closed her eyes and counted to ten. When she opened them, Naomi herself was standing across the street in a canary yellow smock-dress of some kind, with black and white striped stockings. She was wearing clunky yellow clogs and had the unmitigated gall to wave at Abby. She even smiled!

Abby realized in a flash that she was looking directly at the owner of IHAB, Ltd. And IWGY, Inc. It had to have been Naomi all along, scheming and smirking at her across the street and all the while Abby had no idea. And Naomi mean-spiritedly chose the same day to open her store. Abby had spared no expense in promoting the grand opening of the Book Box. It turned out, Naomi was now going to benefit from the money Abby had spent to make sure a crowd of shoppers would show up at the Book Box. These same shoppers, Carmen's shoppers, would undoubtedly cross the street to browse—and buy—at Naomi's new store.

Naomi must have been purposefully sneaky about her comings and goings, because neither Jessica or Mona had said anything about seeing Naomi going in or out of the mystery building. And Abby sure hadn't seen her. She could ask Carmen, but then she realized that Carmen had never met Naomi.

Naomi had played her next card. How many more were coming? Now that she was a multi-millionaire, she would have unlimited resources with which to torture Abby.

But Naomi didn't have *everything* going for her. She obviously had no fashion sense, whereas Abby dressed and carried herself as if she had walked off the pages of a fashion magazine. So, there was that.

She looks like Big Bird in that horrible yellow get-up, Abby thought to herself, and couldn't help but laugh.

≈

Abby decided not to tell Carmen about Naomi's little stunt, and she headed next door to help with the final touches. She wasn't at all surprised to see Carmen already busy in the brightly lit store, walking from table to table, shelf to shelf, adjusting and arranging, making sure everything was just right.

Abby used her own key to let herself in, and when the little bell on the door jingled, Carmen jumped.

"You scared the bejesus out of me," Carmen exclaimed, laughing happily. "What are you doing here so early?"

Abby smiled and hugged her friend. "The same thing you are," she said. "Now put me to work. What else needs to be done?"

The two worked side-by-side contentedly, straightening and fussing, even though everything looked almost perfect already. Carmen took some photos and posted across social media that it was almost time for the big grand opening. Immediately people started to share and like the posts. Abby double checked to make sure the point-of-sale inventory system was online, and then checked her watch for the third or fourth time. The minutes were ticking by as slow as molasses. There were still thirty minutes until show time when Ken arrived at the back door, reporting for duty, and Carmen let him in.

Ken looked so handsome standing by the makeshift bar and beverage station in his flannel lined blue jeans with the plaid cuffs turned up and red plaid lumberjack shirt, ready to pour Mimosas and fresh ground coffee with a steady hand. She watched as he straightened a pile of cocktail napkins with "The Book Box" emblazoned on them. She gave him a finger wave and he blew her a kiss.

Just then, the front door opened, and Abby realized she had forgotten to lock the door behind her. When she turned to tell the visitor that they weren't open yet, she was surprised to see Telly standing at the front of the store, a huge picnic hamper in one straining hand and a folding table in the other. Abby thought she couldn't remember a time she had seen him outside of the Inn, besides when he and Mona delivered breakfast to the ice fishermen, as was their annual tradition.

What was he doing here? She didn't have to ask.

Telly nodded at her and then at Carmen. "Hello," he said quietly, but looking past Abby in Carmen's direction. "I thought you might want some extra goodies for the festivities," he said, holding up the basket. "There was so much leftover Thanksgiving food and I hated to see it go to waste," he added.

"That was so nice of you, Telly," Abby said, reaching out to relieve him of his obviously heavy load, but Telly walked right past her and handed it instead to Carmen, who blushed instantly. Abby tried to suppress a giggle. *So that's what's going on.*

He quickly folded out the legs on the table and flipped it up into place beside the beverage station. There was just enough room. He produced a tablecloth from under his jacket, and he snapped it in the air to spread it out and laid it softly across the table. "Here," he motioned to Carmen, giving her the sweetest of smiles. "Just put the basket here on the edge of the table."

Carmen did as instructed, and Telly began to unpack everything. "I have some delicious rolls that need to be topped with a spoon of the gingered cranberry," he explained. "I also made mini mashed potato muffins with cheese and thyme, sweet potato muffins, and pumpkin tarts."

Out came a much-abbreviated selection of Mona's silver serving dishes and serving utensils, and Telly expertly and artistically arranged the food, even producing a fistful of fresh parsley for garnish. "I also made lemon bars," he added shyly, and Abby watched as Carmen blushed again.

"I hope you can stay," Carmen said. "I'd love for you to take a bow for the wonderful treats."

Telly shook his head. "I'm afraid I can't. Dinner won't make itself. We're bursting at the seams with guests. Best of luck today. I'm sure you will do great," he assured her, taking his leave with the empty picnic basket.

"There's something about that man," Carmen said as the bell jingled signaling Telly's exit. "I just can't put my finger on it. What's his story, besides what Mona said about saving him?" Carmen asked, putting air quotes around the words 'saving him.'

"He's had an interesting life, I will say that," Abby replied, fussing with a stack of children's books. "But I think I'll let him tell his own story."

Abby didn't want to start a long, drawn-out conversation just then. The shop was about to open, and she wanted them both to be focused. And Naomi's new store was very much on her mind.

Unexpectedly, Abby was surprised that butterflies had taken up residence in her stomach as she watched Carmen flip the closed sign to open, raise the blind, and open the door, inviting the group of customers waiting on the sidewalk into the store. It had been just over a year since Abby dove headlong into entrepreneurship, and she was extremely grateful for the success of the Paper Box.

I bet my collection of designer shoes was the difference maker, she joked to herself. *And back then I had an assistant,* she remembered fondly, and the butterflies turned to anxiety. *I wonder how much longer Carmen and I can get by without any help?*

Before joining the Wander Creek police department, Sam Nelson had been Abby's right-hand man, even though she was an attractive and capable young woman. Sam had been Abby's confidant and had helped her navigate the nuances of living in a small tourist town, as well as helping her navigate her own web of secrets. Abby was delighted that Sam was pursuing her passion, but Sam's departure left a big hole in the store, and in Abby's heart. Abby had become very fond of the young woman and liked to think that through her mentorship she had passed on to Sam the kind of confidence in herself and in her abilities that Carmen had passed on to Abby.

Returning from her journey into the past, Abby was delighted to see Carmen making the rounds, checking on the early bird customers. Suddenly the store was full to almost overflowing. Booklovers shrugged out of their coats and hung them on one of the several coat racks that stood throughout the store, or held them in their arms as they perused the shelves.

"Where's contemporary fiction?" someone asked, and Carmen, rather than pointing, led them to that section.

"I hope you have a lot of romances," said Grace Jacobson, the local librarian, to no one in particular. "I just love romances," she then whispered directly to Abby, who proceeded to lead her to a substantial romance shelf near the back of the store.

"Quite right, dear," the librarian praised. "Probably best to keep the steamy stories at the back. And to have champagne in the morning, such a delightful surprise," she exclaimed, beckoning to Ken that she would most definitely appreciate a mimosa. Abby's butterflies eased.

Abby loved how Carmen had arranged the store, with lots of room to browse the shelves and the display tables without the store seeming too crowded. The specialty tables were particularly popular. A group of women, all wearing bedazzled sweatshirts, gathered around the table of suggested gifts for the men in your life. Abby recognized them instantly as the Dazzle Dames, hunting and fishing widows who descended annually on Wander

Creek and pampered themselves at the Wander Inn while their husbands clomped around in the ice, snow, and cold.

Carmen came to stand beside Abby. "By the end of the evening I think I'm going to have to order more stock, at the rate things are going," Carmen whispered, delighted.

They watched the Dazzle Dames scoop up almost all the books on the table until they were all holding stacks of the classic novel *Call of the Wild,* blank hunting and fishing journals with covers of stunning wildlife photography, and a lavish coffee table book depicting gorgeous scenes of Lake Superior.

"Guess I need to get to the sales desk," Carmen said, doing a little dance and snapping her fingers. "I can't believe I forgot to get some sort of shopping baskets for the customers."

"Making a mental note," Abby said as Carmen followed the Dazzle Dames.

I'll get some and we can divide them between the Paper Box and Book Box, Abby thought, her mind whirring with ideas.

Throughout the morning, Abby noticed Carmen was aglow. And she seemed elated. *We are turning out to be a great team,* Abby thought, looking around at more than a few of their fellow merchants, a good smattering of her Wander Creek friends, and a healthy number of tourists. Within the past half hour, the guests had devoured Telly's gourmet appetizers, and only one bottle of champagne remained.

Abby went toward the back of the store where Carmen was finishing a sale at the desk, and handed her a full champagne glass, then tapped a pen against her own glass flute.

"Everyone, can I have your attention please?" Abby said in a strong voice, and the crowd went silent.

"Speech," someone yelled.

"Not a speech," Abby laughed in response, "because I am speechless. I'm speechless at this wonderful turnout for the opening of the Book Box, which I know will be a huge success, because it will be managed by my dear friend, mentor, and one-time boss, Carmen Walker."

The crowd clapped and cheered, and Carmen came around the sales desk to stand by Abby.

"Thank you, Abby," she said. Then she turned to the gathered customers, and said, "And if your support of the Paper Box is any indication of success, I think the Book Box is in good hands. Let's raise our glasses to new friends and new endeavors."

As they raised their glasses to choruses of "hear, hear!" the door swung open with a flourish and Mona whisked in, her entry announced by the tinkling of the bell, which seemed to tinkle a bit more joyfully for Mona than anyone else. She was proceeded by a wave of strong perfume, but just like everything else about Mona, the perfume was luxuriously pleasant, and just skirting the border between marvelous and outrageous. Dressed in an impeccable navy-blue wrap dress, matching heels and an almost absurd measure of sapphires draped anywhere and everywhere, Mona did know how to make an entrance. After years in an unhappy marriage to a member of the English aristocracy, who spent the years neglecting and ignoring her, Mona figured she deserved all the happiness she could possibly gather in her golden years.

Mona finger waved at Abby while blowing a kiss at Ken, then engaged one of the town council members in a conversation about the construction of her new boutique hotel. *That woman is a force of nature,* Abby thought.

When she made her way over to Abby, Mona linked her arm through Abby's. "Take me to the woman of the hour," she commanded, practically pulling Abby to the sales desk.

Uh, oh, thought Abby, bracing herself for another passive-aggressive tennis match. But she need not have worried. Mona was for some unknown reason on her best behavior.

"Carmen," she began enthusiastically, "you've done a wonderful job bringing this little bookstore back to life. I applaud you. I know Abby apprenticed under you at your stationery shop in Minneapolis, and now I know where she got her flare. Congratulations."

Other than the reference to the 'little bookstore,' Abby felt that Mona was being genuine in her praise.

Carmen beamed. "Abby and I make a good team, don't we Abby? Before too long there might even be a third in Abby's box chain. How does the Beauty Box sound?"

Uh-oh, Abby thought again.

"Well, dear," Mona began, "you don't want to compete with the Beautiful You salon, now do you? How about the Sewing Box? You could sell fabric remnants and sewing notions like they do at the craft store in Two Harbors."

To her credit, Abby decided, Carmen brought that turn of the conversation to an end and instead said brightly, "I'm sorry that you missed out on Telly's nibbles. He's a wizard with leftovers, and the crowd devoured every crumb."

Abby cringed. This was not good. Carmen telling Mona how great Telly was? Why was it that anytime these two women came together there were fireworks of some sort?

"I must do some shopping," Mona announced. "I'm looking for some coffee table books of the local area to put in the guest rooms at the Inn," and she flounced off, refusing to even acknowledge that Telly had even been there earlier that morning.

To Mona's credit, she did end up buying eight of the Lake Superior coffee table books, and she and Carmen seemed to have shared a friendly moment as they admired the stunning photographs in the book, agreeing that they were spectacular.

By noon, it was clear to Abby that Carmen had everything in hand. *She has ten times more experience in this than me*, Abby mused, anxious to return to her cozy shop and get it opened for business.

As the afternoon progressed, in between her own customers, Abby poked her head out of the front door and watched as shoppers flowed back and forth between Naomi's new store and the Book Box, many of them carrying glossy yellow shopping bags bearing a firefly, which apparently was Naomi's logo.

Abby had purposefully refrained from telling Carmen about the new store across the street opening the exact same day, and probably minute, that the Book Box opened. Surely Carmen had been too busy chatting and ringing up customers to notice anything across the street. *Hope she didn't notice any of those stupid yellow shopping bags with the stupid little firefly. I will tell her at the end of the day anyway,* Abby promised herself.

The end of the day came, and Abby was going through the normal ritual of closing the store. The deep north woods darkness had already descended upon the town, but the streetlights illuminated the front of the buildings. As she reached to pull down the blind on the front door, she paused to glare across the street at Naomi's competing stationery store, and realized, for the first time, that the woman had spelled the word 'stationery' incorrectly. And even worse, there was an extra 'O' in 'book.' The phrase on the awning clearly read, "Naomi's Stationary and Boook Store."

CHAPTER 8

*S*till tickled by Naomi's misspelled store sign, Abby let herself into her apartment and waited for Carmen to join her for a debrief.

Carmen let herself into the Paper Box with the key Abby had given her, locked the front door behind her, and made her way up to Abby's apartment. As the exhausted pair, especially Carmen, lounged on the comfy couch, they chatted about the day, about how strong sales had been, and about all the important people who had attended the grand opening, and both were pleased with what could only be described as a remarkable success.

Finally, Abby decided to bring up Naomi's store. "Did you notice that mystery store across the street opened today, too?" she asked Carmen.

"Yeah, I noticed," Carmen said. "And it's a stationery and bookstore, too."

"Certainly is," Abby replied, trying to remember how much she had told Carmen about how evil and annoying Naomi was.

"What's a little competition between enemies?" Carmen asked wickedly, sipping a glass of Abby's favorite Merlot. "And judging from the spelling, or should I say lack thereof, on her awning, I doubt she can remain a woman of letters for very long." She held up her glass and clinked it to Abby's. "Let's drink to the Book Box and the Paper Box and forget about Naomi."

"Long may they reign," Abby said, more than a little concerned that Naomi's store would in fact be a big drag on her businesses.

"Have you actually talked to her?" Carmen asked. "Wouldn't it make it easier if you just went over there and said hello and welcomed her to the business community?"

"Welcome her back, you mean," Abby said, reminding her that Naomi used to own and operate the Beanery coffee shop and bakery, which was now under new, and much better, ownership. "I'm not sure that's such a good idea. Besides, I have a ton of stuff I need to get done at the Paper Box, and there is Christmas to plan for."

Abby was already sick of Naomi, and decided it was time to change the subject. "Let's talk about how much Telly is into you," she said, giggling mischievously.

Carmen blushed and took a long sip of her wine to avoid addressing the issue of Telly. "I'm sure I don't know what you're talking about," she eventually said, looking anywhere but at Abby.

"Oh, dear," Abby said, "you're going to be difficult. Well, never fear, I'm here to break it down for you." She held up her hand and began ticking off her fingers. "Number one, Telly served you first during Mona's welcome dinner and called you the guest of honor."

"I kind of was, wasn't I?" Carmen argued.

"Don't interrupt," Abby said, continuing. "Second, the two of you were smiling goofily at each other the second were introduced. And third, he brought treats, unsolicited, to the grand opening of the Book Box, and gave them directly to you.

And he made the lemon bars especially for you. He was probably up all night making everything."

Carmen guffawed.

Abby ignored her, "And fourth..."

"Fourth, nothing," Carmen said. "I want to go back and talk about Naomi. Even though I am not afraid of a little competition, someone should go inside and take a look around."

"I certainly can't do it. She hates me," Abby said. "She'd probably call the police. And she knows Jessica and I are friends so if we sent Jessica that would be awkward," Abby said. "Why don't you just go over? She doesn't know you from Adam. Or from Eve."

"And be the welcome wagon?" Carmen asked. "I'm afraid she'd take a bite out of me. From what you've told me about her, I just don't know. Nope. It has to be someone else."

The two women looked at each other and began to think hard until suddenly they said simultaneously, "Mona."

After Carmen left, Abby enjoyed another glass of wine and reminisced about the Paper Box's grand opening just a few years before, and how well it had gone, thanks to the new friends she had made. And that made her think about Pete White, one of Wander Creek's two letter carriers, who was so instrumental in everything that had happened to bring Abby to Wander Creek in the first place. Abby wished he could have been here to celebrate her accomplishments at the Book Box. She wanted him to be proud of her. But he and his lady friend, Sarah Beth, had already booked a cruise vacation and made plans to see Sarah Beth's family in California for Christmas. Abby knew Pete was disappointed to miss the grand opening. Just then Abby's phone buzzed with an incoming call. From Pete.

Abby answered the call and Pete asked, "How's my favorite girl doing?"

~

As the days progressed toward Christmas, Abby and Carmen remained careful not to order the same sales items, and to do their best to keep things exclusive to each store. They both knew it wouldn't serve either of them if the two stores were too similar. Abby had moved her stock of local attractions books to the Book Box. In fact, the Paper Box no longer carried books at all. On the musical soundtrack in the Paper Box, Abby chose to play upbeat, modern music, while Carmen decided on soothing classical music that would not distract book browsers. Each store had its own distinctive feel, and Abby liked that.

Abby knew she needed help running the Paper Box, and although Carmen had the Book Box humming along nicely, it was obvious to Abby that she needed another person too. But hiring two people would be so expensive. And what if you hired the wrong people? Then you had to figure out a way to get rid of them, and then you had to start the process all over again. The whole idea seemed like a huge hassle.

As she walked to the Inn, after being beckoned by Mona, Abby tried to convince herself that she could make it on her own at least a little while longer.

Jessica was already sitting in Mona's private apartment when Abby arrived. Although Mona had beckoned them as if they were schoolgirls bound for the principal's office, she had also invited them to enjoy a late cold supper with her. Telly entered bearing a large serving tray stacked high with scrumptious cold cut meats and cheeses, a variety of fruits cut in interesting shapes, homemade breads, and delicate Russian tea cookies dusted to perfection with powdered sugar. Jessica, always the brave one, snatched a cookie from the tray and shoved it into her mouth just as Telly handed around the plates and napkins.

"Phank ye," Jessica said with her mouth full, under Mona's

disapproving gaze. Jessica did have the grace to cover her mouth and sink back into her chair to avoid further scrutiny.

"It has come to my attention that I have the solution to a problem you both share," Mona announced.

Jessica and Abby exchanged looks, and Jessica finished swallowing her cookie.

"I wasn't aware that you were aware that we had a problem," Abby quipped.

"Of course I know that you do," Mona said, exasperated, as if Abby and Jessica should know exactly what she meant. "Between your three shops you are terribly understaffed. I propose that you hire one full-time sales associate to float between the three stores. She or he will learn the different sales systems and inventories in no time. Their schedule might vary from day-to-day, but they would be a full-time employee with a full-time salary."

Abby's heart quickened. This was actually a wonderful idea. Abby, Carmen, and Jessica could stagger their lunch hours so the shops wouldn't have to close. And it would be easy for the new employee to run between the three shops in a matter of seconds since they were so close to each other. If they hired someone at the assistant manager level, they could even take on more responsibilities and hold down the fort for longer periods of time. This could work! *Maybe I can take a vacation!*

"Mona, you are a genius!" Abby said, jumping up to hug her friend.

"Of course, I am," she responded with her tinkling laugh. "I'm surprised you didn't already know that.

"I'm in, too," Jessica said. "I assume I would only be paying one-third of this person's salary because they would spend two-thirds of their time working for you, Abby."

"That seems fair. We can work out the details later, but first let's start the hiring process."

Mona waved her hand in the air, the way a queen might

dismiss her subjects. "You don't have to worry about that," she said.

"And why is that?" Abby asked, afraid of Mona's answer, knowing the unconventional way Mona hired her own staff.

"Because the perfect person will arrive at the right place at the right time and be the exact right person for the job."

Jessica and Abby again exchanged looks but knew better than to convey any hint of doubt in their glances.

"Any idea of when this might happen?" Abby asked, playing along. "Now that you've suggested we hire and share a full-time employee I am more than ready to get started."

"Darling," Mona drawled, "if I knew that I would have already told you. Now chop, chop. You two have a lot to do to get ready for your new employee, and I have a photo shoot to prepare for."

Before Abby could utter the words, "What photo shoot?" Mona had ushered them out of her private apartment, past the well-appointed front parlor, through the lovely foyer, and out onto the front porch.

"How does she do that?" Jessica asked.

"Which part?" Abby quipped. "Insert herself into our businesses even though she has her own business to run, or scoot us out of the way until before we know it, she's closed the door and we're out in the cold?"

"Both, I guess," Jessica laughed.

∽

Abby could not stop thinking about Mona's odd statement about a photo shoot. It was unlike Mona to have something big going on and not tell everyone about it. So Abby made an impromptu visit to the Wander Inn a few days later. She loved the short walk down Main Street, even if it was a frigid December day.

The town leaders, as well as the shopkeepers, always went out of their way to make the town a Christmas paradise. Beautiful strings of colored and white lights crisscrossed above the streets of the business district, and window frames were adorned with gorgeous garlands, ribbons, and decorative embellishments. Shopkeepers decorated their stores inside and out with all the trimmings of the season, and often good-naturedly competed with each other to see who could make the most creative display window. The town's public works department hung banners and garlands on the light poles all along Main Street, Hickory Street, Maple Lane, and Wolf Path Lane. Before too long, the snow piles would get higher and higher, further adding to the charm of Wander Creek. Abby loved every minute of it. Christmas in Wander Creek was the opposite of the dazzling whirl of Christmas parties she attended in her former life, where everyone tried to outdo each other with how much money they spent on gifts and decorations. Christmas in Wander Creek was real.

When Abby arrived at the Inn and entered the large wooden doors into the front foyer, she was surprised to see Mona standing just inside, as if she were expecting someone.

"What are you doing?" Abby asked Mona.

"Nothing," Mona said, examining an imaginary piece of lint on her suit jacket.

"Uh, huh," Abby said. Mona Sixsmith never did *nothing*. Everything the woman did had a purpose. If Mona was up to something she did not want Abby to know about, that could not be good.

"If you're not doing anything then you won't mind if I hang around," Abby said, trying to bite back her delight. "Maybe we could sit in the solarium. I do so like looking over the frozen creek. Maybe we'll see some skaters."

"It's too early for skaters," Mona practically snapped. "The ice won't be safe until January or February."

Just then the front door opened and a neatly dressed young woman carrying a leather portfolio entered the lobby. She seemed somewhat surprised to see a welcoming committee.

"Hello," she said enthusiastically. "I'm Lauren Jones here to see Ms. Sixsmith about the job opening at the Paper Box and Book Box. Oh, and the Life and Style boutique."

Abby gave Mona the side eye and saw her friend cringe at the young woman's pronouncement. Mona obviously did not want Abby here. But Mona did not miss a beat.

She held out her hand. "I'm Mona Sixsmith. Delighted to meet you." She turned to Abby. "And this is Abby Barrett, the proprietor of both the Paper Box and the Book Box." Mona said this as if Abby's presence had been planned all along, instead of being a serendipitous coincidence. "Let's conduct the interview in the dining room, shall we?"

As Abby and Lauren followed Mona, Mona stopped at the registration desk and pulled out two legal pads and two pens from the counter, handing one to Abby and keeping one for herself, as if this was what she had intended to do all along.

How does she do it? Abby wondered. *Even when she's totally busted, she makes it look like she isn't.*

When the three settled at the massive dining room table, Abby decided to take charge. This was a prospective employee for her shops. She would deal with Mona's presumption later.

"Miss Jones, please tell us about yourself," Abby began.

But before Abby knew what happened Mona had taken over the interview, and suddenly it was over. Lauren made her exit, and Abby turned to Mona. "Well, what do we do now?"

"We have three more candidates coming. One is probably waiting in the lobby as we speak, and we don't want to keep her waiting."

"Mona," Abby said gently. "Why all the cloak and dagger stuff?

I thought you said the perfect person would arrive at the right time?"

"Don't be angry with me, dear. I'm just a little old lady trying to do a favor for a friend in need. I've seen how frantically you're running between the two shops. And poor Jessica is almost always late picking up her son from school."

"Yes," Abby agreed. "Did you know they charge parents an additional fifteen dollars for each minute they are late?"

"That's preposterous. Jessica must be losing a fortune. You just leave that to me. I'll drop a small fortune in her shop next week and that ought to ease her financial pinch."

How could Abby be angry at Mona after that generous gesture? She had to hand it to Mona, she knew how to play a scene to perfection and how to end it with a flourish.

It turned out that there really were three additional candidates, but one quickly rose above the rest. Emma Rose had recently followed her husband to the area when he took a new job with a manufacturing company in Two Harbors. They lived just ten minutes outside Wander Creek. Emma had experience managing a university gift and bookshop in Ohio.

They chatted amiably about the three shops on Main Street and how the schedule would work. Emma was warm and friendly and seemed the utmost professional. Abby liked her at once. She guessed Emma was in her late twenties or early thirties. She was dressed conservatively in a grey suit but sported a bright pink blouse underneath. *She will be the best of both worlds,* Abby thought, *dependable and creative.*

Abby smiled widely as she shook Emma's hand at the end of the interview, welcomed her profusely to the area, and said they would be back in touch soon.

"What did you do that for?" Mona asked once Emma had left the Inn.

"Do what? What did I do?"

"Let her walk out of here without hiring her," Mona said, as if this was the most obvious thing Abby would ever hear.

Abby looked incredulous. "But you always have to check references before you hire someone, unless you already know them. That's just standard procedure."

"Poppycock," Mona said. "I've never once checked references on any employee. I go on gut instinct and right now my gut is telling me to tell you to hire that woman before someone else does!"

As always, Abby did as Mona instructed.

I guess my gut instinct tells me to follow Mona's gut instinct! she thought as she hurried out of Mona's apartment and out into the parking lot to catch Emma before she left for good.

CHAPTER 9

*N*ow that Emma was on board, and despite Naomi's ongoing nastiness, Abby was surprised by how relaxed she felt. Yes, it would take a bit of time to fully train Emma to work in the three shops, but the young woman was extremely capable and obviously knew a lot about running small retail stores. She was up to speed almost immediately. It was going to be a win-win. *Even a win-win-win,* Abby thought.

The next afternoon during a lull in business at the Paper Box, Abby dialed Jessica's cell phone. "I think it's time to infiltrate Naomi's store," she said.

"Past time," Jessica agreed. "I really cannot believe Naomi. Nothing has changed. What do you have in mind?"

"Meet me at the Bistro at seven tomorrow evening. I'll tell Mona we want some more advice about something, like I don't know, maybe hiring another person. That would certainly pique her interest. Plus, she may be a gazillionaire who wears ten-thousand-dollar dresses, but she can't resist a good basket of piping hot buffalo wings."

Abby sent Mona a vague text about needing her opinion

about something urgent and important and Mona responded with her customary formality:

"Dear Abby. This is Mona. Of course, I will come, dear. Let's sit at our usual table and have some of those yummy gourmet wings."

In the meantime, Abby had some important online shopping to do, and she did not even mind the shipping fees she would have to pay. It would be well worth it to see what Naomi's store looked like.

~

Abby and Jessica arrived at the Bistro right at the appointed hour, with Mona making a dramatic entrance ten minutes late. Abby watched as her fellow patrons craned their necks to get a glimpse of Mona as she weaved her way through the tables to join her and Jessica. *Always the showstopper, that woman,* Abby thought.

"Oh, there you are girls. I am so sorry to have kept you waiting, but you know how busy and important I am." This was followed by dramatic hand flourishes and tinkling laughter.

Mona took her seat, orders were placed, and drinks and appetizers appeared in front of them.

Abby moved quickly from small talk to the topic at hand. "Now that we've followed your advice and hired Emma we have another little project for you," Abby said to Mona.

"And it's right up your alley," Jessica chimed in. "Remember last year when you wanted to hire a retired FBI or CIA agent to spy on the man playing the saxophone across the creek that turned out to be Marcus? Well, it's sort of like that."

"Except," Abby said, trying to make the whole thing sound exciting and mysterious, "you would be in the role of the agent."

Mona took a long sip of her martini and then helped herself to a boneless buffalo wing, nibbling it in an impossibly ladylike manner, all without taking her eyes off her dining companions.

"Go on," she said.

Abby quickly explained that she needed Mona to go into Naomi's store wearing a hidden camera so she could get a good look at the interior.

"Why don't you just break in during the middle of the night like you did at the warehouse?" Mona suggested.

Abby gave Mona an exasperated look. "Can you just imagine what Naomi would do to me if I were caught. If she didn't kill me, I'd go to jail for sure. And believe me, I wouldn't do well in jail. Or the military, come to think of it."

"Can we please focus?" Jessica implored them. "You're going off on tangents. First things first." She brought out her phone and tilted it so all could see, scrolled through the online shopping site Abby had showed her, looking at the various models of spy cameras hidden in all kinds of items, such as eyeglasses, hats, handbags, and even jewelry.

"Give it here," Mona said, grabbing the phone. "I can't see a thing on this tiny screen. Now, let me see if I have this right. You want me to go in and wear a baseball cap or sunglasses and walk around Naomi's store recording what I see, and then deliver the recording to you? Surely you must realize that I have never worn a baseball cap. And I'm quite certain I never will." She looked at Abby. "Besides, I've already been inside Naomi's store. And don't start with me. Naomi may be a crazy mean girl, bordering on psycho, but she is still a guest at the Inn."

Abby knew that Naomi *was* psycho. "I know you've been in the store, but that was before it opened. You yourself said everything was still in boxes. And of course we don't want you to wear a baseball cap or sunglasses. Keep scrolling. There are necklaces that you can wear, and the camera would be front and center. It looks like a pretty pendant."

"Sort of like the position of a police officer's body camera," Jessica piped up helpfully.

Mona helped herself to another wing with fingers that were impossibly clean while continuing to scroll with her other hand through the hidden camera jewelry options on Jessica's phone.

"These are all hideous, as far as jewelry goes. Let's suppose I was going to do this—and I'm not saying I'm going to—but if I were to, I would have to have a piece of jewelry custom-made. I could never wear any of these ... these ... things," she finished, waving the phone in the air.

"Mona," Abby said softly, taking the phone and handing it back to Jessica. "You are overthinking this. We are talking about ten minutes tops. We buy one of these necklaces, you wear it along with some of your real jewelry and walk around the store. That's all there is to it."

Mona paused dramatically. "Oh, all right," she finally said. "I do like a good caper now and then. Now let me see those necklaces again. I will choose the least abominable option."

"No need," Abby said, opening her own phone. "I've already ordered something. It will be here tomorrow." She thumbed through her photos and brought up a screenshot of an orb-shaped pearl pendant on a gold chain.

"Putting aside your audacity in assuming I would play along, this one actually isn't terribly offensive," Mona said. She tilted Abby's phone. "If I look at it just right, it almost resembles the pearl embellishment on one of my Coco Chanel handbags."

Abby and Jessica burst out laughing, which elicited a very small grin from Mona.

～

*N*ow that Mona was fully engaged with the caper, Abby didn't waste any time. The hidden camera necklace arrived the next day, and in between customers she read the instructions, examined the device carefully to familiarize herself with its workings, and installed the necessary app on her phone. The feed would be recorded into the cloud, and then Abby could download it onto her phone or laptop. She also watched a few YouTube videos so she would be sure that she placed the camera on Mona in just the right position so that she wouldn't be tempted to fiddle with it, perhaps telegraphing what she was up to. Abby practically rubbed her hands together with glee.

Fortunately, it was Wednesday, the day that Naomi stayed open until eight. Abby texted Jessica and Mona with the plans and suggested they meet at Jessica's store so Naomi wouldn't see them across the street.

"Yes, that was a good idea," Mona said, when the three were assembled. "Definitely don't want a staging area too close to the subject."

"Oh, brother," Abby laughed, "we've created a monster."

"Don't be silly," Mona answered. "I've always been larger than life. But despite what people think I am not one hundred percent unflappable, and I am a little nervous that I'm going to make a mistake, as preposterous as that sounds."

Abby explained the workings of the camera to Mona and Jessica and helped hang the necklace over Mona's head, carefully arranging it among the many diamond and pearl necklaces Mona already wore.

"See?" Abby said, bringing a compact from her purse and holding it up so Mona could see herself. "You can barely even notice it with all the other jewelry around it."

"Well high thanks for small mercies," Mona said, smoothing one of her eyebrows with a pinky finger. "I couldn't bear it if I ran into anyone I know wearing this horrible bauble." She fingered the necklace.

Abby gently hit her hand. "No. Don't touch it. First of all, if you move it then you might jeopardize the line of site, and second, if you draw too much attention to it Naomi might get suspicious."

"Oh, all right, stop fussing," Mona said. "Can I please go now? I want to get this over with."

"Yes," Jessica said, "and remember, ten minutes, and be sure you move around the whole store and stand back far enough so we can see the store from many angles. And if there is anything particularly bad then try and get a close up."

Mona adjusted her purse. "Is that it? Am I free to go?"

"We just want to make sure it goes okay," Jessica said apologetically.

Without answering, Mona turned on her expensive boot heel and headed to Naomi's store.

"What do we do now?" Jessica asked.

Abby set up her laptop on Jessica's desk in the small office at the back of the store, connected to the wireless and brought up the website where she could also download the recording from the hidden camera. It gave her a little thrill to know that anytime she wanted to, she could look at a recent recording of Naomi's store on her phone or computer, and Naomi would never know.

"We wait," Abby answered.

~

An excruciating forty-five minutes later, Mona finally returned to Jessica's shop.

"Honey, I'm home," she tinkled.

"Where have you been?" Abby scolded, coming to meet Mona at the door.

Jessica was right behind Abby and locked the door after Mona entered. "We've been worried sick. We thought something had happened to you!"

"Moi?" Mona asked innocently, taking off her suede and fur coat, which she had promised not to button up lest she accidently bump the camera. Then she sat down dramatically in the only comfortable chair.

"Well?" Abby asked. "Did it work?"

Mona took off the necklace and handed it Abby. "I guess we'll find out."

Abby opened the app on her phone, clicked on the spy camera pendant, and video began to play.

Jessica clapped her hands and did a little dance. "It worked! Here, let's watch it up on your laptop so we can all see."

Abby typed a few keys and then turned the laptop around.

"You were in there for a very long time," Abby pointed out.

"I had a lot to say," Mona responded.

"Not about us, I hope," Jessica said.

Mona gave her a sideway glance. "Of course not. I happened to run into a few guests from the Inn and had to make small talk and introduce them to Naomi and blah blah blah. And then Naomi wanted advice about running a bed and breakfast, which she is determined to put into that old warehouse."

"Can we please just watch the video?" Jessica implored, and Abby hit the space bar and the images started moving.

"Wow, this is really clear," Abby said. "And the audio quality is unbelievable. Nice work, Mona."

"Did you expect anything less from me? And might I add that I think you will be pleasantly surprised at what she has done with the place."

They heard Mona greeting Naomi and saw Naomi turn her cheek for what they presumed were Mona's customary air kisses.

Naomi began to speak, and a chill ran down Abby's spine. She turned down the volume on the laptop.

"I can't stand to hear her voice," she explained. "Plus, at this point I'm only interested in what the shop looks like. But if Naomi said anything I need to know, please tell me."

On the laptop screen, it was clear that Mona started strolling around the entire store, making a circuit.

"Now here is where I wanted to make sure I got a wide shot of the entire store," Mona explained.

On the laptop screen, the women watched as the camera captured, one by one, the walls, sales counter, display tables, bookshelves, and even a beverage station.

"And here is where I made sure that I got every inch of the place," Mona said. "I did it like a grid, you know, how law enforcement searches for clues on television."

"You didn't get the floor," Abby pointed out.

"Oh, no? Fast forward through the next twenty minutes when I'm talking with the guests."

Abby did as she was instructed and sure enough, Mona must have been down on her hands and knees, because there was Naomi's floor.

"I pretended that I had lost a contact lens," Mona said with glee, "so I could look all over the floor. Now I know you told me not to touch that ugly pendant, but it was swinging out back and forth while I was crawling around down there. So, I had to hold it still. And, by the way, you owe me a pair of Givenchy black leggings. That floor was so disgusting! As soon as I get home, I'm throwing this pair out."

Neither Jessica nor Abby responded. Abby had rewound the video and slowed the replay so they could see Mona's first circuit around the store again.

"Eww, it does look dirty," Jessica observed. "It's as if she hasn't dusted anything. How could it get so dirty in just a few weeks?"

"I'm more interested in her displays and what she's selling,"

Abby said. "Let's fast forward to the displays and zoom in on them."

Abby hit the fast forward button until the first display table came into view, then hit play.

"What is that?" Jessica asked. "Is that what I think it is?"

"Yep," Abby said. "It's exactly what she did with the Beanery display window when she owned it. She didn't want to decorate for individual holidays, so she displayed decorations for all the major holidays all at once. It was like a freak show. Pilgrims standing next to little green elves and paper hearts dangling over ferocious looking monsters."

The three focused on the display table near the front, practically crumbling under the weight of Christmas decorations, Saint Patrick's Day decorations, and decorations seemingly intended for Thanksgiving, Valentine's Day, and Halloween, all jumbled together.

"I must admit that I gave her a few pointers," Mona said. "The place is just a shambles and I felt sorry for her."

Abby rolled her eyes. "Let's just keep looking."

With the volume turned down, Mona took that as an invitation to continue as narrator. "This table here—Abby, pause it please. This table here actually had a delightful selection of stationery items for home and office. You can see the pretty patterned notebooks, colorful file folders. Even the staplers are nice."

"But what's that leaning up against the bottom of the table?" Jessica asked.

"That, my dear, is the Easter Bunny," Mona explained with a straight face Abby could not understand how she held.

The video continued around the display tables, then Mona walked slowly along the bookshelves, pausing long enough to capture some of the book titles.

"Those books aren't in any order, are they?" Abby asked.

"Not that I could tell," Mona said. "I may not be a big reader, but I know enough that you don't put Ernest Hemingway next to a book about mountain bikes."

Having had enough of Naomi's dreadful store, Abby thanked Mona for her service, and bid her and Jessica farewell. She headed back over to the Paper Box and was very grateful to be safe and sound in her apartment, and to sink into her couch in front of the cozy gas logs. Her mind was whirring with all that she had just seen. She almost felt sorry for Naomi. Then she remembered Naomi's venomous rage. There really was something wrong with that woman. And Abby knew deep in her soul that Naomi had returned to Wander Creek for one reason only—just to punish Abby for whatever transgressions Naomi believed she had committed.

After a well-deserved glass of wine, Abby changed into her snuggly leggings pajamas and top and slid into bed, her body instantly feeling better. Then she remembered she owed Mona a pair of Givenchy leggings. *Maybe I'll give them to her for Christmas.*

Abby picked up her phone from her nightstand and googled "Givenchy leggings." She clicked on a link that took her to one of the most exclusive and expensive department stores in the country. And Abby was very familiar with this department store, because she used to shop there herself. She gasped as she viewed the price. Those leggings were five-thousand-dollars. Even when she was married to Jake and seemingly had unlimited wealth, she would never have spent that amount of money on a pair of leggings.

I sure hope Mona was kidding about those leggings.

CHAPTER 10

With only two weeks left to go before Christmas, both the Paper Box and the Book Box were beautifully decorated for the season. There was no room for a Christmas tree in the Paper Box, but an oddly placed alcove in the Book Box provided just enough room for one. Instead of a tree skirt, Carmen stacked books around the bottom of the tree to hide the stand, and then placed wrapped gifts in front of the books. Tree decorations included bookmarks and ornaments in the shape of books, in addition to traditional ornaments and fairy lights.

Attracted by the deepening snow, snowmobilers and cross-country skiers had invaded the area, many staying at the Wander Inn, and enjoying the trails and tracks all along the creek and beyond in the great northwoods. The majority of the rental cabins in the surrounding area were booked up till the New Year. Several guests were from out of state and were in the area for the fantastic ice sculpture and light festival in Duluth. Faithful to the end, these folks always chose the Wander Inn, despite the three-hour round-trip drive to Duluth. And many Duluth day-trippers loved coming up to Wander Creek for the day, many making the trip almost weekly throughout the fall and winter. They all loved the feel of Wander Creek.

Abby loved the cozy feelings Christmas evoked. The familiar decorations brought her joy. She had done her share of decorating at the Paper Box, with lots of wrapped boxes lying about the store and stockings stuffed with pens and notepads and greeting cards hanging here and there. She hung a beautiful garland made of cedar and gold tinsel all around the store. The shelves were all embellished with strings of lights, and she arranged small nosegays of pine, berries, and ribbons on the display tables.

She had hoped to create a new window display this year, but with the opening of the Book Box, she hadn't had time, so she recreated the previous Christmas display with a large rag doll sitting at a table writing a letter to Santa. A cute paper mâché dog slept at the doll's feet, and all around were wrapped gifts. The rest of the window was decorated with lights and stationery items hanging from clear fishing line. The final touch was a large red mailbox labeled "Letters for Santa."

The decorations in Abby's apartment were subtle and cozy. She brought out Christmas throw pillows and pine-scented candles. She loved to decorate with bowls, and put handfuls of pinecones in one pretty glass cut bowl and silver and gold glass balls in another, placing them pleasingly in the living room and dining room respectively. She decorated her mantle with evergreen, magnolia leaves (courtesy of Mona who had them flown in for her own decorations), and red ribbons. She was still thinking about buying a stocking for Ken.

Now that Emma Rose was in place, making the rounds between the Paper Box, Book Box and Jessica's shop, Abby was free to do the creative things she loved about owning her own business. With Emma staffing the sales floor for a few hours,

Abby began setting up for that evening's Christmas card deco-rating workshop. All the shelving and display tables that were not attached to the walls were on wheels. Abby rolled them all off to one side of the store, but they were still accessible to shoppers. She put up two round folding tables for the ten people who had registered for the class.

She was particularly excited about the mahogany Lazy Susan turntables she purchased in Two Harbors for the center of each table. After dressing the tables with festive green and red striped tablecloths, she placed the round turntables in the center of the tables and loaded them with supplies galore: cut-outs of Christmas and winter scenes, scraps of colored paper, rice papers and knobby textured papers that looked handmade. Next to those she placed markers, stickers, colored pencils, all sorts of little embellishments, die cuts, and a plethora of clever little Christmas flourishes. She also included rubber stamps of Christmas trees, poinsettias, and holly, red and green glitter and colored glues. She had found a box of vintage Christmas cards while on a trip to Duluth and she divided them up between the two tables. Each table had a stack of folded blank cards with envelopes—the blank canvasses for the evening's creations.

Promptly at six, people began arriving for the workshop. Emma took their coats and they assembled at the tables, chatting and laughing amongst themselves. They were a festive group and Abby could tell it would be a jolly time.

Abby greeted Grace Jacobson, Wander Creek's librarian, who attended every workshop, a few other locals, and the rest out-of-towners, probably guests at the Wander Inn.

Abby was no longer a rookie at these workshops, and she cringed when she thought of the first workshop she held. She had prepared a thirty-minute PowerPoint presentation on the history of letter writing, which bored the audience so much she was sure a few of the attendees fell asleep. But she couldn't resist injecting a little bit of history after she welcomed the current group and thanked them for coming.

"Before you dive in, just a little bit of history," she promised. "The tradition of sending Christmas cards is said to have started in England in the 1840s," she said enthusiastically, skipping the next seventy-five years. "But it took until 1915 for the modern Christmas card to take off when they were manufactured en masse by the Hall brothers of Kansas City. They would go on to found the company Hallmark. Now, let's get decorating!"

Her audience seemed to appreciate the tidbit about the Hall brothers, and were quick to dive enthusiastically into the materials there at their tables. Abby was admiring Grace's work when she looked up and was surprised to see Telly hovering at the store entrance looking around. When he saw Carmen, who was also participating in the workshop, his face lit up like a Christmas tree. Abby smiled to herself. Suddenly, things were getting interesting.

"Do you have room for one more?" Telly asked Abby, coming into the store.

She had never seen Telly in anything but his chef togs and she couldn't help staring. He looked so different in khaki pants with razor-sharp creases and a light blue oxford dress shirt under a dark blue sweater. Abby didn't look, but she figured Carmen must be gaping at him, too.

"We certainly do have room," Abby said. "Why don't you sit here next to Carmen, and I'll just grab another chair." The person next to Carmen slid her chair over to make room for Telly to sit. "It's my night off," Telly told Carmen. "I thought it might be fun to do something new."

Uh-huh, Abby thought. *You thought it might be fun to do something new . . . with Carmen.* Abby had to resist bursting into song and singing "Carmen and Telly sittin' in a tree, k i s s i n g."

Halfway through the workshop, a cold wind blew through the store as the door to the shop opened. Abby hadn't locked it since her workshop attendees would be leaving soon, and she figured surely the "Closed" sign would keep people out.

She looked up just in time to see Naomi Dale stomp into the shop, face red, arm raised with a pointed finger. Abby was startled to see Naomi in the flesh just a few feet away. This was the first time since Naomi's return that they were seeing each other in person, rather than just glaring at each other through their shop windows.

"I want to talk to you, Abby Barrett," Naomi screamed.

Abby winced, getting déjà vu from the first time she and Naomi had met. She looked over to the far wall and the greeting card display. It had been right there, in fact. And Naomi had been yelling just as loudly. Would this never end?

"Naomi," Abby whispered, "please keep your voice down. We're in the middle of a workshop. I'd be happy to talk to you later, when we're done."

"NO, NOW!" Naomi demanded, and she stomped toward the back of the store and into Abby's private office. Abby figured she didn't have any choice but to follow.

Abby closed the office door and said in a whispered hiss, "I've had just about enough of your outbursts and carryings on. You have two minutes to tell me what you want and then leave my store."

Naomi leaned against the desk, her black jeans, faded sweatshirt, and stringy dyed blonde hair standing in stark contrast to Abby's beautifully coifed hair and dark green pantsuit. Even Naomi's innocent ankle boots looked worn and torn next to Abby's elegant Queen Anne's office chairs.

"I can't believe you did it again," Naomi said, resuming her finger pointing. "You haven't changed a bit."

Abby was tempted to say, "Neither have you," but bit her tongue. The trick to dealing with Naomi was not to engage. And Abby had already done that by allowing the woman into her office. Not that there was much she could do to prevent it, other than removing her bodily from the premises, which she certainly wasn't going to do.

"Naomi, I'd like you to leave. Now."

But Naomi did not listen and barreled on. "You hired yet another employee out from under me."

"What on earth do you mean?"

"Emma Rose, that's what I mean," Naomi shouted.

"Emma didn't mention that she was working for you during our interview or when I hired her, so I fail to understand what exactly your problem is," Abby said smoothly, trying very hard not to lose her temper.

Both women turned at the sound of footsteps as Emma let herself into the office.

"Everything okay in here?" she asked. "We can hear the yelling even with the door closed," she said, pointedly staring at Naomi. "And I heard my name, so I thought I'd better investigate."

Bless you, Abby thought.

Naomi did drop her voice a bit but then turned her venom on Emma. "I was going to hire you for my shop. I just hadn't gotten around to it yet. I have a friend who works with your husband who told my friend who told me you were looking for a retail job. And now look what happened. Abby stole you out from under me, just like she did with Sam, the first person she lured away from one of my stores."

Emma emitted a small chuckle, which turned into a side-splitting laugh. "I'm sorry," she said, wiping tears from her eyes. "It's so funny to hear you say you 'hadn't gotten around to it yet.' That's the craziest thing I've ever heard. And it's just too, too funny. I think I might pee my pants."

Suddenly, Naomi was quiet, and she stared open-mouthed at Emma, who continued to laugh hysterically.

"This isn't the end," Naomi warned as she stomped away. "I'll be back."

"She sounds like something out of bad action movie," Emma said, starting to laugh all over again.

As soon as Naomi was gone, Abby burst out laughing too. "You were awesome. I can't believe you got her to leave."

"It's nothing I did, really," Emma said, her laughing under control. "She's just so ridiculous I couldn't help it."

For the rest of the evening, Abby and Emma made the rounds of the tables, answering questions about the materials and commenting on each person's decorative flair. Each participant could make as many cards as they wanted and at the end of the evening would leave with a goody bag of green and red pens and Christmas gift tags.

As she was talking to a woman at Carmen and Telly's table, Abby overheard the tail end of a conversation. Carmen was saying, "I would love to, Telly. That sounds so delightful."

Obviously, plans had been made. Carmen and Telly were finally going on a date.

As Abby watched six-foot-tall Telly and five-foot-nothing Carmen leave the Paper Box, she pondered the power of love, its soaring highs and sinking lows, its power to propel people across oceans, and then cross them again. She was thinking, of course, of Elise and Dennis. And then there was the matter of her love for Ken. They weren't quite on the same page, but they were working together on the same book.

After putting the Paper Box back to rights and thanking Emma for staying late, Abby walked up to her apartment and went directly to her bedroom.

Not knowing what else to do with the paintings, Abby had carefully placed them in the back of her closet. It didn't seem right to hang them. They were so intimate and obviously meant as a gift between two people in love, if what Marcus said was true. She had no reason to doubt that it was. Abby felt she should keep the paintings private, even from herself. It was true that she had found the paintings on property she owned, so by legal rights the paintings were hers. But really, there could only be one owner, and that certainly was not her. She just could not decide if they belonged to Dennis or to Elise. Wouldn't it be nice if they could reunite with each other, and enjoy the paintings together, as they had so many years ago? Until that happened, she would make sure they were safe and hidden, just as Dennis had done so many years ago.

CHAPTER 11

"I feel like a schoolgirl," Carmen said as she fussed with the finishing touches of her make-up in the bathroom of Abby's apartment. "And I haven't set foot in a school for about forty years, so there's that."

Carmen wore a long-sleeved burgundy A-line dress that complemented her short stature. She wrapped a colorful scarf around her shoulders like a shawl and pinned the ends together with a gold circle broach.

Abby gave her an encouraging smile. "You look beautiful and confident. There's nothing to worry about. You like Telly, right?"

"Are you sure you and Ken don't want to double with us?" Carmen asked, coyly avoiding Abby's query. "I'm sure Telly made enough food for four, or probably more, knowing him."

When Abby didn't respond, Carmen turned to look over her shoulder to face her.

"What?" Carmen asked. "And are you actually blushing? You're up to something, aren't you?"

"No," Abby lied. "Of course not. What would I be up to?"

Carmen turned back to the mirror and smoothed down her

glossy black hair. "Well, whatever it is, I just don't want to know about it or be embarrassed by it. Deal?"

Abby felt relieved and gave her friend a dazzling smile.

After saying goodbye to Carmen and watching out the apartment window as Carmen let herself out the front door of the Paper Box and climbed into her Mini, Abby grabbed her coat, hat, scarf, and purse and ran out of the back door and down the alley, checking often to make sure Carmen or her Mini was nowhere in sight. Abby then turned right onto Maple Lane and headed hurriedly toward the Inn. As instructed by Mona, she dashed around to the back and slipped in through one of the service entrances. Mona loved a little cloak and dagger and intrigue now and then, and she had told Abby the precise time she would have the door unlocked and had instructed Abby that she must not be late.

Breathless from her brisk walk, Abby entered Mona's apartment, and found her fiddling with what looked like a baby monitor.

She stopped short, peeling off her coat.

"You seriously did not put a bug in the dining room," she said to Mona. "How could you?"

"Well, it is my Inn, and Telly is my employee."

"Aren't you invading his privacy? And Carmen's?" Abby argued, taking a seat next to Mona on the couch.

"Not at all. I provided him with the private dining room for this, whatever it is, date, I guess. I even paid to hire a sous chef for the week to help him get ready for it," Mona offered in her defense.

"Nonsense, you hired someone for the holiday season way before Carmen arrived in Wander Creek," Abby reminded Mona.

"That's beside the point," Mona said, pouting.

"I can't even remember what the point was," Abby said, accepting a glass of wine from Mona. She stared at the baby monitor on the table in front of them. "Yes, the point. That it is a huge invasion of their privacy to be spying on them."

"Ssshhh," Mona commanded. "I hear them."

Abby abruptly reached over and switched off the monitor.

"What on earth did you do that for?" Mona asked.

"The only way I will go along with this is if we agree that once they start talking about personal issues, or begin to talk about either of us, then we immediately turn it off," Abby said.

"What constitutes personal in your mind?" Mona asked. "Can we listen to them talk about their childhoods, but not, for example, about past relationships?"

"Don't be difficult," Abby commanded, and she switched the monitor back on. "I'll be in charge of the switch so whatever I decide goes. And the only reason I am staying is because if left to your own devices I'm certain you'll make a mess out of this."

Mona crossed her arms over her chest and whispered, "That will have to do, I guess. Now be quiet so I can hear what they're saying."

This was the last thing Abby thought she'd be doing tonight. When Mona invited her to spend some time with her at the Inn during Telly and Carmen's date, she thought perhaps they might listen at the door for just a minute, or interrupt them during dessert just to say hello. Had Abby known about Mona's hijinks she would have stayed home.

"Thank you so much for inviting me, Telly," Carmen's voice came over the monitor. There was a pause, and Abby thought she heard Camen's footsteps as she walked into the dining room. "Oh, my goodness." Carmen's voice again. "This is so beautiful. The flowers, the appetizers, it's amazing."

Mona suddenly piped up so neither of them heard Telly's response to Carmen.

"Uh-oh," she whispered. "I hope Carmen doesn't look too closely at the flowers. I put the microphone in that big arrangement on the buffet. Actually, I practically doubled the size of the arrangement to disguise it."

"Oh, geez," was all Abby could manage.

"I suggested the menu," Mona whispered, even though no one could hear them, and certainly not Telly and Carmen, who were all the way on the other side of the Inn.

Telly's voice crackled on the plastic speaker. "We'll get things started with this charcuterie board. I selected an assortment of cheeses, figs, dates, and there's a baked camembert topped with pistachios and honey."

"This is amazing," Carmen said.

Abby assumed that they were done with the appetizer when Telly announced that the next course would be sweet potato soup.

"This soup is delicious," Carmen said, her voice rising above the clink of antique silver soup spoons against expensive china. "I've never had a sweet potato soup so delightfully peppery, and is that a hint of sage I taste?" More clinking spoons. Telly said something low and unintelligible, at least to the eavesdroppers. Abby imagined the painfully shy Telly smiling into his bowl.

"Sweet potato soup!?" Mona exclaimed indignantly. "What happened to the creamy squash soup I personally recommended? It was to be served with shaved walnuts. And a swirl of luscious cream."

"Well, like you said," Abby replied, "you suggested the menu, and I guess he just ignored your suggestions. What are they having for the entrée?" Abby asked. "Or, should I say, what did you suggest?"

"What better for a crisp fall evening than pork chops topped with baked apples?"

Abby tried to hide her surprise at Mona's choice of entrée. "Pork chops? That seems kind of basic for a chef of Telly's talents, don't you think?"

"I was thinking for a woman of Carmen's age and station that she would be delighted with pork chops. Pork is a staple food, you know."

Oh no, here we go, Abby thought to herself. It all came back to the rivalry between Mona and Carmen. And what did pork chops have to do with Carmen's age anyway? Abby herself liked a good pork chop, but for a first date she herself would serve maybe a pork roast or baked chicken and save the pork chops for the second or third date. This feud was getting out of control.

Small talk and clinking silverware hissed out of the baby monitor. Carmen asked Telly if he had made the sourdough rolls himself. He said that he had and gave her an abbreviated explanation of sourdough starter. She expressed enthusiasm and he promised to show her how to bake a loaf.

Mona rolled her eyes and sighed dramatically, "I guess that means Carmen will be spending more time over here, distracting Telly from his work."

"So, Telly's sixty hours a week isn't enough?" Abby asked pointedly, ignoring the evil eye Mona cast her way.

The sound of a chair scraping along the floor was followed by what sounded like a serving dish being set on the table.

"I hope you like Beef Wellington," Telly said in a voice that was strong with a pride and certainty and that Abby had never heard before.

"Beef Wellington?" Mona screeched. "He hasn't even made that for me! It's a huge undertaking."

Abby suppressed a smile as she imagined Telly slaving over the pastry in the kitchen, with visions of Carmen dancing in his head.

"I adore Beef Wellington," Carmen said, her delighted voice coming out of the monitor. "It's been years since I've eaten it though, and yours smells more scrumptious than any I've had before."

"It's all in the cut of meat and the quality of the pâté," he said.

"And I like to make the individual servings because I can better control the way the meat cooks."

More clinking of silverware.

"And to accompany the beef I have asparagus with hollandaise sauce, and herb roasted baby Yukon potatoes. But be sure to leave room for dessert."

Mona stage whispered, "I told him peach cobbler. Everyone likes a good peach cobbler."

Abby suspected that not to be true, and her suspicion was confirmed when Telly said, "Voila, a Baked Alaska. I made one portion. Hope you don't mind if we split it."

"I can't think of anything I'd like more," Carmen said coquettishly,

Abby stole a glance at Mona, who, if she were not so proper and elegant, would probably have stuck a finger into her mouth and made exaggerated gagging noises.

And Abby decided that what they were doing was just wrong. *I can't believe I am actually eavesdropping on Carmen.* Abby grabbed the baby monitor from the coffee table and switched it off.

"Okay, that's it," Abby said firmly, slipping the speaker deep into her purse. "We've been spying long enough." She rose to leave, blowing Mona a kiss as she donned her outerwear.

"And where do you think you're going with my monitor?" Mona asked indignantly.

Abby turned the handle on the door to Mona's suite and opened the door. "I'm saving you from yourself. You can thank me later."

Abby enjoyed the short walk home and laughed aloud as she thought about Mona and the baby monitor. She did feel somewhat guilty about the whole thing, not just because she, too, had listened in on a private conversation, but because she thought she had probably put the idea in Mona's head in the first place with the hidden camera shenanigans they had carried out at Naomi's shop.

CHAPTER 12

"*I* need to see Mona," Abby declared when she came into the Wander Inn in a huff. She felt like she had just been here, probably because she had. Her conscience had been nagging at her and she had to set things right.

Abby followed Lorna, the new young front desk clerk, down the hallway to Mona's private apartment.

Lorna, in her conservative navy-blue pantsuit, her gorgeous red hair braided into a long ponytail, knocked on the door. "Miss Sixsmith, Miss Barrett is here to see you."

Despite their close friendship, Mona insisted upon formalities as much as possible, and Abby had gotten used to them.

Abby couldn't help an eyeroll behind Lorna's back.

A muffled voice came from within, and Lorna opened the door and stepped aside, saying, "Miss Sixsmith will see you now."

Abby thanked Lorna, suppressing another eyeroll. It wasn't poor Lorna's fault that they had to go through this ritual.

"What a nice surprise," Mona said. She was sitting at a small desk, a laptop in front of her, and she was wearing a leopard print wrap dress with matching heels. Her jewels, Abby observed, sparkled a brown color that matched perfectly. *Where did she get these things?* Could you dye jewels to match your outfit? Abby made a mental note to google "brown gemstones."

"I've come to talk about our bad behavior," Abby announced to the room.

Mona rose and beckoned Abby to sit on the luxurious chintz couch in front of the fireplace and she took a seat beside her. Abby always felt frumpy around Mona, though she was wearing her best jeans and a silk blouse, but she obviously had to wear her snow boots for the walk over.

"Now what is this about bad behavior? What have you done now?"

"*Me?*" Abby practically screeched. "Not me. *Us.*"

"Whatever could you mean?" Mona said, looking Abby straight in the eyes.

"You know very well what I mean," Abby said, trying to bite her tongue. "The more I think about it, the worse I feel about how we invaded Carmen and Telly's privacy."

"Phsaw," Mona said, waving her hand in the air. "How is that any different than the stunt you pulled spying on Naomi?"

"The stunt *we* pulled," Abby said pointedly.

"Yes, but you bullied me into it, so I am just an innocent victim."

"Oh, cut the crap," Abby said. "We've both behaved badly. But since you asked, spying on Naomi, who has dedicated her life to ruining me, is far different than helping ourselves to a private conversation between our respective employees." Abby huffed, took in a deep breath and leaned back, her hands crossed over her chest. "And Naomi's store is open to the public and recording is not illegal in the state of Minnesota. Or at least I don't think it is."

"What's done is done," Mona said dismissively. "All we can do now is not do it again. Unless you're suggesting that we make some grand confession and apologize to Carmen and Telly."

"Of course not."

"Well then, that's settled," Mona said, concluding the conversation. "Was there anything else? I really need to get back to work."

Abby glanced over at Mona's laptop where she saw a screen full of dresses on an online shopping site.

She looked back at Mona. "Actually, there is. While we're on the subject of bad behavior, why haven't you invited Carmen to your annual Christmas dinner?" Abby asked, incredulous at Mona's oversight. Abby was really picking up steam, but Mona didn't seem to notice. Or care. Mona had the uncanny ability to exist in whatever world she created for herself, typically deflecting all conflict or blame away from herself. This could be charming, but Abby was not the least bit charmed in this moment.

"I just assumed she would have relatives or friends back in Minneapolis to spend the holiday with," Mona said.

"She does," Abby said, "but she is so committed to the Book Box that she wants to make sure she's in the store for Christmas Eve shoppers and for the after Christmas sales. And of course, there's New Year's Eve."

"What could a bookstore possibly do to celebrate the New Year?" Mona said.

"You'd be surprised," Abby answered. "And I guess you'll just have to stop by to find out. You might want to consider starting with a clean slate with Carmen in the New Year."

"What could you possibly mean? I am always polite to everyone I meet. Sweet as pie."

"Yes," Abby agreed, "but despite being an impeccable hostess, you are picking fights with Carmen, like a junkyard dog, and trying to keep her and Telly apart."

"I beg your pardon," Mona said indignantly.

Mona looked away from Abby, uncharacteristically lost for words.

"Marcus said the same thing to me a few days ago, so I suppose you're both on to something."

"What do you have against Carmen anyway?" Abby asked, glad that she had finally found the right time to broach the subject with Mona.

"I think it has something to do with the fact that she is really short and doesn't dress well," Mona said, matter-of-factly.

While Abby appreciated Mona's directness, this was going too far and nowhere at the same time. Mona, who rescued stray people, like Telly, took them in, gave them jobs, was judging a stranger by her height and fashion sense?

"That seems really outrageous, even for you," Abby responded, trying to sound neutral, which was the exact opposite of how she felt.

"I honestly don't know," Mona said. "She just rubs me the wrong way. I took an instant dislike to her, and I don't know why."

"That's exactly what Carmen said about you," Abby quipped.

Mona's eyes widened in surprise. "You're not serious?"

"I had this conversation with Carmen right after your welcome dinner." Abby used air quotes around the word welcome. "And she said almost word-for-word about you what you just said about her."

"I can't believe you would talk to her about me," Mona said.

"Why not?" Abby asked. "We're talking about Carmen now and we talked about her all through her first date with Telly."

"That's different," Mona insisted. "Us talking about her is a whole separate thing."

"How's that?"

"Well," Mona sputtered. "I'm not sure yet. I'll have to think about it and tell you later."

"Can't you two just try to make things work. I love you both dearly and I want the three of us to be friends. Would you please invite her to Christmas dinner?" Abby almost pleaded.

"I'll think about it," Mona said. She then quickly added, "Oh, very well, if it's that important to you. I'll send her a text."

"You don't have her cell phone number," Abby pointed out. "You'll call on her at the Book Box and extend the invitation personally and warmly."

Mona gave Abby the evil eye but agreed.

It seemed a good time to bring up another dimension of her relationship with Carmen.

"Does this have anything to do with Telly?"

"Of course not," Mona snapped.

Abby couldn't help but notice that Mona protested a little too much. Of course, this was tied to Telly's attraction to Carmen, at least partly. Abby would have to find another time to broach that subject with Mona. Arriving unannounced and taking Mona by surprise seemed to be a good strategy. *I must surprise her more often.*

∼

Abby decided to keep her meeting with Mona to herself, but it didn't matter because when she popped into the Book Box later that day, Carmen greeted her with a cheery, "Guess who I just talked to?"

"I have no idea," Abby said, trying not to sound guilty.

"Sure you don't," Carmen said, "but I forgive you and now I'm looking forward to Mona's Christmas feast. If I know Telly, and I think I do, I'm sure it will be one of the most incredible meals I've ever eaten."

"What about all those gourmet food trucks in Minneapolis that you raved about during your welcome dinner?" Abby teased.

Carmen had the decency to blush. "Mona started it," she pouted.

Changing the subject, Carmen moved to the front window where Abby was standing, peering out towards the enemy. They watched as Naomi exited her store lugging a sidewalk sign that read "Half-Off All Inventry." Naomi paused at the door, and noticing Abby and Carmen, gave them a rather rude gesture involving a particular digit of her hand. Then she put down the sign and repeated the gesture for good measure with her other hand.

Abby sighed. "She really needs to learn how to spell. Even her ads in the Duluth newspaper have misspellings. I guess her radio ads are okay, but only because she doesn't need to know how to spell."

"What do you think it's all about?" Carmen asked. "It's crazy to drop prices right before Christmas. This is the top income-generating season."

"I don't know what she's up to, but so far she hasn't hurt our business, though it's probably too soon to tell what, if any, long-term effects her shenanigans will have. Who knows what else she might have up her sleeve."

Just then, Naomi emerged from the store again with a second sidewalk sign that read, "Buy One Book, Get Three Free."

"Well, look at that," Carmen said. "She actually got the spelling right on that one."

"What the heck is she up to?" Abby said, now starting to get a little worried.

Naomi repeated her earlier gestures before disappearing into her store again.

Within minutes, cars started appearing on Main Street as if arriving for a special event. They all parked as close to Naomi's as possible and a steady stream of customers headed into her store all day.

"What was that I said about it being too soon to tell?" Abby asked. "Maybe I spoke too soon." She sighed. "The only consolation is that her store is a total mess and some of her inventory looks used. It kind of reminds me of a thrift store."

Carmen, who was arranging a pile of books, stiffened, and Abby knew instantly that she had made a mistake. Uh-oh. She had not wanted Carmen to know that she and Jessica had enlisted Mona's help to infiltrate Naomi's store. What if she slipped again and Carmen found out she and Mona had eavesdropped on her first date with Telly?

"Why, Abby Barrett," Carmen said, turning, a sly smile spreading across her face. "You bad girl. You did something totally, deliciously wicked and didn't include me, much less tell me about it."

Sheepishly, Abby said, "I didn't want you to think less of me."

"Less of you?" Carmen said. "You must remember that it was me who talked us into going into that warehouse."

"That was different," Abby said. "It was just the two of us and not so . . ." she groped for the word, finally settling on, "underhanded."

"Do tell," Carmen gushed. "I want to know every little detail. Don't leave anything out."

"Well, the story sort of involves Mona. Want me to leave her out?"

"Especially don't leave out anything about Mona," Carmen said.

Abby hoped Carmen wasn't thinking something along the lines of, *It would be nice to have something to hold over Mona's head.*

It took most of the afternoon for Abby to tell Carmen the story of Mona's secret camera excursion because they kept getting interrupted by Naomi's customers. Almost without fail, customers would exit Naomi's and head over to the Paper Box, and then the Book Box in turn.

"If she's not careful she's going to go out of business," Carmen said. "She's giving away her inventory and then sending her customers over here to actually spend their money."

"I don't think so," Abby lamented. "She's got all that lottery money to invest in the store."

"I wouldn't be so sure about that," Carmen responded. "Haven't you seen those TV shows that document how people who win the lottery overspend so much and before you know it their winnings are gone and they're destitute in just a year or two?"

"Mmmm," Abby said, but she wasn't really listening. She was trying not to delight in overhearing yet another shopper complaining about Naomi's store.

"Did you see those bookmarks?" one woman asked her friend. "I swear I saw dirty fingerprints on them." Then she scooped up a handful of Carmen's bookmarks and headed to the register.

This went on all afternoon in both stores.

"I don't think that woman knows anything about books."

"I feel like I need a shower after being in that place."

"I think some of the pen and pencil sets she's selling are used. Did you see those fake Parker pens?"

At the end of the day, when most of the shopkeepers on Main Street were bringing in outside signs and displays and locking up, Abby felt an overwhelming desire to walk across the street and stand in front of Naomi's grimy window and yell, "Na-na, na-na, boo-boo," while sticking her thumbs in her ears and wiggling her fingers.

Maybe another time.

CHAPTER 13

*I*f Abby was going to successfully play matchmaker with Elise and Dennis, she needed to act fast. Christmas was only two weeks away. Abby picked up her cell phone and tapped out the phone number she found handwritten on a manilla envelope in the pile of sales documents from when she bought Pages bookstore from Dennis. After the third ring, a familiar voice answered, "Hello?"

"Hi Dennis," Abby said cheerfully. "It's Abby Barrett."

"Abby!" Dennis exclaimed. "How are you? I don't think we've spoken since you bought my business."

"I think you're right," Abby replied. "All is well here in Wander Creek. You know, same old same old. So, forgive me, I can't remember where you retired to."

"I'm in Florida now. Love it down here. I bought a two-bedroom condo on Anna Maria Island, right on the gulf coast. It's got everything. Pool, tennis, dog park, you name it."

"Sounds wonderful," Abby said. "So, are you enjoying retirement?"

"Absolutely. I love it. But I stay pretty busy buying and selling books online. Mostly rare editions, things like that."

"Do you miss Wander Creek? Ever consider coming back for a visit?" Abby asked.

"I do miss it some, but I never really thought about visiting. I guess when I left, I considered myself leaving for good," he explained.

Abby decided it was now or never. "Remember Mona's famous Christmas feast at the Inn?"

"Of course," replied Dennis. "I was honored to be on the guest list every year."

Abby continued, "Well, I was talking with Mona just the other day, and we were reminiscing about last year's dinner, and discussing who she was going to invite this year, and your name came up."

"My name?" Dennis asked, obviously surprised.

"Yes, we were saying how fun it would be to catch up. And I'd love to show you what we've done at the Book Box. We built upon your strong foundation. I think you'd really like it."

There was a moment of silence, and Abby thought and hoped that Dennis was really considering a Christmas visit to Wander Creek.

Eventually Dennis began to speak. "I don't know, Abby. You know the weather can be treacherous for travel around the holidays. And it's such a long haul. I think I better stay in Florida, where it's warm and sunny."

"I understand your hesitance, but surely there will be a day or two of clear weather when you can travel. I am sure Ken would be happy to pick you up in Duluth and drive you the rest of the way up," she said, not wanting to take no for an answer.

"I don't know Abby. I just don't think it's a good idea. I'm flattered that you and Mona thought of me, but I'm gonna have to pass," he finally decided.

"Well, I must say I will be very disappointed if you can't come," Abby said, knowing this was the right time to lay it on thick. "You see, Dennis, although the Book Box is doing okay, and Carmen is great and all, I just have this gnawing feeling that we are not living up to our full potential. As a business, I mean. I was really hoping you could give the store a once over, kind of like an unofficial audit, and point us in the right direction. A man of your obvious business acumen, and years of experience and accumulated knowledge in the bookselling business, well, surely you can see why someone like me would want someone like you to offer his advice and recommendations. Your opinion would be invaluable."

"Wow," Dennis responded. "You make me sound smarter than I really am."

"Now Dennis, don't sell yourself short."

"Look, Abby, I would be happy to consult with you or Carmen anytime by phone," Dennis offered.

"I don't know, Dennis. I think you should really be here in person to get the full picture of what's going on," Abby explained.

Dennis continued to resist, and they spent the next few minutes chatting about Dennis's online book business. After Dennis assured Abby for the third time that he was definitely not coming for Christmas, Abby politely ended the call.

Abby picked up her wine glass from the island, walked over to the couch, and plopped down with a big sigh of disappointment.

I'll wait a couple days, then I'll call him again. I'll keep up the pressure, but not make it too obvious.

Abby was getting sleepy, and she stretched out on the couch and adjusted the pillows on the armrest. She closed her eyes and let her mind drift, and a vision appeared of Elise as a young and beautiful woman, painting the man she loved more than anything in the world as he napped against a tree, an open book propped against his chest. She was rudely jolted from her reverie when her phone rang.

It's so late. Probably just Ken calling to say goodnight, she thought.

She grabbed her phone from the end table and was shocked to see it was Dennis calling.

"Hi, Dennis," she said enthusiastically, sitting upright on the couch.

"Hi, Abby. Sorry to call you back so late. I've been thinking about your invitation."

"And?" Abby prodded.

"Well," Dennis began, "I don't really have any family down here, or anywhere, for that matter. And all my Florida friends are going to their kids' places for Christmas. So, I was thinking I might try to come to Wander Creek after all."

"That's wonderful, Dennis," she said, trying not to let her exuberance show through too much. It still was not a definite commitment though. She still had a little work to do.

"You know how particular Mona is about her Christmas guest list. So, can I tell her to put you down as a *definite?*"

There was a long, silent pause, and Abby imagined Dennis weighing the pros and cons in his mind. Finally, he spoke the words Abby wanted to hear. "Yeah, tell her to put me down as a definite."

～

After giving Carmen all the details from her discussion with Dennis, Abby finished by saying, "I just love seeing so much love everywhere, you and Telly, Mona and Marcus and now maybe Dennis and Elise."

There was a lull in customers at the Book Box, and they did not expect a crowd for at least fifteen minutes, which was about the time a group of shoppers spent in Naomi's store before heading over to the Book Box and the Paper Box.

"And you and Ken?" Carmen asked, looking frankly at Abby.

"Don't think I haven't noticed how little time you're spending together. Is something wrong?"

"Of course not," Abby said, busying herself with a fleck of fluff on her sweater. "I have been really occupied with two businesses. Or should I say two successful businesses." Abby gave Carmen a shoulder hug, transitioning the conversation from Ken to Carmen. "And that's in large part because of you."

Carmen smiled tightly and looked around the store as if seeing it for the first time.

"It is, isn't it?" she said, almost wistfully. "I'm proud of the work I've done here. It's been a tremendous challenge, but a good one."

Abby noticed that Carmen hadn't said anything like, "I love managing the Book Box and I want to stay here forever," or, "Time to put my condo on the market and look for a house in Wander Creek."

Abby realized that she did not know if Carmen had been out of Wander Creek since she had arrived. *I really should have taken her to Duluth for lunch and an afternoon out.* But Abby had just been so busy with the shops and preoccupied with Ken and that stupid little black velvet jewelry box.

"After Christmas things will slow down and you'll have a chance to explore the area," Abby said. "Duluth is a lovely and very cultural city and there are fun things to do in Two Harbors, like a climbing wall place that also does escape room parties."

Carmen smiled tightly. "That would be fun."

Her body language said otherwise.

"Now that we have Emma on board, maybe I'll take a weekend to go to Minneapolis," Carmen pondered. "If you're okay with it, that is."

"Of course," Abby said, suddenly realizing she had to do a better job of making sure Carmen was happy living in Wander Creek. It hadn't occurred to her that Carmen might miss the city and all its amenities. When Abby first arrived in Wander Creek it was a relief to be away from Minneapolis and all the bad memories, and she had settled in quickly, making friends like Jessica and Mona. She winced when she thought of Mona's distinctly hostile behavior toward Carmen. How much that must have hurt Carmen. Abby had to do better.

On the other only hand, it's only been six weeks, Abby tried to reassure herself. *We haven't even gotten through Christmas yet. And then there's Telly . . .*

∼

With the first phase of Operation Dennis and Elise implemented, Abby, Jessica and Mona met at the bar at the Bistro to discuss strategy and scenarios.

The bartender had just served them their crab stuffed mushrooms. Their drinks had already been delivered, and they immediately began to discuss the upcoming reunion between Dennis and Elise.

"I just hope it's not a total disaster," Abby said.

"What makes you say that?" asked Mona.

"I don't know," replied Abby. "I just feel like when you try to manipulate circumstances to act as a matchmaker, things can go sideways in a hurry."

"Wasn't this your idea?" Jessica asked, staring at Abby.

"Yes, of course it was. And don't get me wrong, we are still doing this."

Mona, in her typical fashion, framed the situation like a business plan. "So what we need to do first is run through some scenarios. Then we can devise an action plan, or more like a *reaction* plan, to each scenario. After that we can decide on plan B, or maybe C and even D if necessary."

"Let's just slow down," Abby said. "Let's just start at the beginning and work through the evening."

"Very well," Mona began. "As previously discussed, Marcus has assured me that he will have Elise at the Inn exactly fifteen minutes before go time. Abby, since you will hopefully be giving Dennis a tour of the Book Box on Christmas day, you can make sure you and Ken deliver him at precisely the right time."

"Okay," Abby said. "I guess it would be helpful to know who else is going to be there."

"Just the usual suspects," Mona said. "Marcus and I, Abby and Ken, Carmen, Dennis and Elise. All the Inn's guests will have their Christmas dinner in the large dining room while we'll be in the smaller private room."

"Sorry you're going to miss this," Abby said to Jessica. "But I know how much you've been looking forward to spending Christmas with Aiden."

"Thanks," Jessica replied, and Abby sensed she might rather be at the Inn on Christmas just to see how things turned out.

Mona got back to business, addressing Abby. "So, you and Ken enter with Dennis. I'm assuming you'll have Carmen with you, too. Let's say that Marcus and Elise are already seated. Elise will be shocked to see Dennis, Dennis will be shocked to see Elise, but both will deal with it. Elise won't get too out of line with Marcus there. And I'm sure Dennis, being as laid back as he is, will be just fine."

"I sure hope so," Abby said, not sounding very confident.

"So what are you afraid will happen?" Jessica asked.

Abby thought a moment before saying, "I don't know, maybe when she sees Dennis Elise will jump up and shriek like a banshee, storm out of the dining room, sprint across the ice on Wander Creek, and not stop running until she gets back to her cabin."

Mona and Jessica guffawed in unison, and Mona said, "Abby Barrett, don't you think you're being a little overdramatic?"

Not wanting to miss out on the fun, Jessica offered her rendition of what might happen. "Or maybe Elise will be so upset to see Dennis she will jump up and pour the gravy boat on his head. And when Mona rushes over to break it up she slips in the gravy, and when she hits the floor, her wig flops off."

Mona shot Jessica a wicked stare, then deadpanned, "The most preposterous element of that scenario is the idea that I would ever wear a wig."

Abby brought them back to reality. "It's just that I want this reunion to turn out, well, perfect. I would love for it to be a happily-ever-after ending."

"Listen. This is what is going to happen," Mona began to explain. "Dennis will be shocked but delighted to see his long-lost love. Elise, likewise, will be shocked but delighted to see Dennis. They will greet each other pleasantly, dine side by side on Wander Inn's legendary Christmas fare. They will enjoy polite conversation with each other, and with us, throughout the evening. They will remember why they liked each other in the first place. When it's over, they'll make plans to see each other again."

"Oh, Mona!" Abby exclaimed. "That's pretty much how I envisioned it!"

Jessica chimed in with her practical take on it all. "Look, whatever's gonna happen is gonna happen."

To which Mona added, "She's right, you know. Look, if it doesn't work out, at least we have tried our best. We cannot force them together."

Abby knew Mona was right, but she could not decide if she felt better or worse after this conversation.

CHAPTER 14

"*A*re you sure I can't persuade you to come upstairs for a drink?" Abby asked Carmen. The two were sitting, exhausted after an influx of Christmas Eve shoppers, in Abby's office in the Paper Box.

"Ken is coming over at nine," Abby continued. "He has some last-minute arrangements to make for a snowmobiling group arriving the day after Christmas."

Carmen slipped out of her heels and rubbed her feet. "I am so glad to be sitting down, you have no idea," she said.

Abby lifted her leg on the side of her desk, revealing her own shoeless foot. "Yes, I do," she said, laughing.

"My feet hurt so much I don't think I could walk up the stairs to your apartment. I might just have to live in your office for a few days. As for your invitation, thank you, but I am going to sneak into the kitchen at the Wander Inn and spend some time with Telly. He has his hands full with tomorrow's dinner. He might even let me help."

"Sneak in?" Abby asked. "As in slipping in the back door so Mona doesn't see you?"

"Something like that," Carmen said. "I feel like a teenager

sneaking out to meet my boyfriend. It's kind of fun. Well, I better get going. I wish I could wear these shoes for my date in the kitchen, but it's got to be flats or nothing."

She rose from her chair and finger-waved at Abby. "Toodle-loo."

Abby hated to admit it, but she felt a little let down to be alone tonight. First Ken had to delay their evening together and now Carmen had a date, which she was thrilled about, of course.

She had decided that it was time to face up to her fears and finally have a serious conversation with Ken about their relationship, her doubts about marriage, all couched with how much she loved him. Although it was likely to happen sometime, she doubted Ken would propose on Christmas Eve when they were both exhausted from a long day of last-minute Christmas shoppers and adventure seekers. He would be wearing his typical jeans, work boots, and plaid flannel lumberjack shirt. And he knew her well enough to know when he arrived she would be wearing the comfy clothes that he jokingly referred to as "one step up from pajamas." Tonight, would be relaxing and easygoing. Just the kind of low-key evening they both needed. She had planned to just lay out a light supper of cold cuts, cheese, and fruit. *The calories we are going to consume at the Wander Inn tomorrow will be enough to sustain us both for a week.*

Leaving the office, she shut off the light and was about to lock the front door and flip the sign and then head upstairs when she heard the bell above the front door jingle and in walked Jessica.

Surprised, Abby asked, "I thought you were spending Christmas Eve with little Aiden?"

Jessica, looking cute as ever in matching pink hat and mittens with a black coat, responded, "He's with my ex until nine so Santa can come and eat his milk and cookies." She laughed. "He'll be surprised tomorrow morning when he sees that Santa had a second helping at my house. Anyway, I got a Mona emergency text just now. Seems she needs a very specific special kind of apple for tomorrow's dinner and she asked me to run to Two Harbors to pick up a dozen. Want to ride along?"

Abby didn't hesitate. "Love to," she said, happy to have something to do.

~

The parking lot was full at the grocery store in the strip mall at Two Harbors. Inside, busy customers were probably frantically looking for last-minute ingredients and decorations, just as Abby and Jessica were. It wasn't like Mona to need anything so last minute. When they entered the store, they veered to the right into the produce section. Abby headed to the bins with the apples.

"What kind does she want?"

"Honeycrisp. A dozen," Jessica said. "And I forgot I need some potatoes, so you get the apples and we'll meet at the checkout. Make sure you look through them very carefully and choose only the ones without bruises or scratches. Mona was very specific about that."

Abby pulled a plastic bag down from the dispenser and did as she was told, wondering why Jessica was acting so strangely. She seemed nervous, fluttering about with her strange instructions. Sorting through the apples and moving aside the ones that did not meet Mona's high standards, she suddenly gasped and held her hands to her mouth, the plastic bag dangling.

Nestled in the apple bin was a small black jewelry box. Just like the one she'd seen Marcus and Ken inspecting at Mona's birthday party.

"I see you found it," a voice behind her said, and Abby whirled around to see Ken, impeccably dressed in a blue pin-striped suit she had never seen before.

He moved in front of her, plucked up the jewelry box and got down on one knee. Tears appeared in Abby's eyes. She put down the plastic bag and clutched her hands to her heart. "Oh, Ken," was all she could muster, thinking she had never loved him as much as she did in this very moment. She noticed that the hubbub in the grocery store had died down and all the shoppers around her had stopped, seemingly in their tracks, to watch. Then she saw Jessica, a mischievous grin on her face, holding up her phone taking photos and recording. Abby looked back at Ken.

Ken opened the box and held it up for Abby to see, revealing a gorgeous princess cut diamond set in platinum.

"Abby Barrett," he said very seriously. "From the moment we met, right here on this very spot, I knew that one day you would be my wife. I can't explain it, it was just a feeling I had, a flash, and then suddenly I knew. Will you make me the happiest man in the world and marry me?"

The shoppers around them erupted with applause, laughter and cheers. Of course, Abby wanted to spend the rest of her life with Ken. She knew that for certain. And here he was, making a grand and vulnerable gesture in a produce section full of strangers. She looked at him, still on one knee, his handsome face beaming up at her, holding out the ring in a most sacred offering. If she waited even a second longer, she knew he would sense that something was wrong. She couldn't do that to him.

"Yes," she said, louder than she thought she would. "Yes, I will marry you."

The grocery store exploded again with applause and hoots and hollers as Ken swept Abby into his arms, and holding her tightly, dipped her toward the floor and kissed her. She clung tightly to him, never wanting to let go.

When they separated from their embrace, he said, "I got the wedding band that matches," Ken said as he slid the diamond onto Abby's ring finger. It fit perfectly.

By then Jessica had appeared by Abby's side, snapping more

photos and hugging Abby and Ken seemingly all at the same time.

"How did you know my ring size?" Abby asked Ken, holding the ring out in front of her.

"I have to admit to some more subterfuge on that one," Jessica said. "Last year, when Ken asked for my advice on the ring . . ."

Abby interrupted, laughing. "I can't believe you knew and kept it a secret all this time!"

"What kind of friend would I be if I ruined the surprise?" Jessica said. "But believe me, it was a hard secret to carry around. Anyway, I snuck into your apartment twice, once to borrow a ring from your jewelry box and the second time to put it back. You really should lock the door to your apartment during the day. Anyone can sneak in there." She was grinning widely.

On the ride home in Ken's truck, he told Abby how he, Jessica, and Mona had planned the proposal. It had been his idea to propose in the grocery store where they had first met. And Mona and Jessica cooked up the part about the apples.

"I wanted to do something romantic," Ken said. "Something memorable. When we first met, you were holding a Honeycrisp apple. I can still see you, examining it as if was the most important thing in the world to you."

Abby was glad to be talking about something other than wedding plans. Her head was spinning from what just happened.

"And you had no idea that I had been dead broke just a few weeks before and couldn't afford to buy an expensive Honeycrisp for the past year."

There was an awkward silence as Abby cursed herself for referring to her first husband, even if it was only peripherally. She wondered how many times she had told Ken her story. Once Jake's Ponzi scheme had been exposed and all their assets were seized, she was left practically penniless, and went from being a rich socialite to someone who had champagne taste on a water budget.

Ken quickly filled the silence.

"Do you know why they are so expensive?" he asked, and Abby shook her head. "I Googled it when I got back to the office that day. I had to know why my future wife was so interested in the Honeycrisps. Seems they are very high maintenance and require specialized care and even with that only about half of a crop makes it to market."

Abby laughed. "You're always full of surprises," she said. "I had no idea you wanted to marry me from the beginning."

"Now the next thing we have to do is set a date, choose a venue, and book the photographer," Ken said. "Both Mona and Jessica have made it perfectly clear that these things must be done immediately or else our plans will be ruined, and our wedding cursed."

Abby laughed. "There's plenty of time for all that," she said. "Let's just enjoy the moment." She held out her hand again. She could not wait to see the ring in the morning light.

Ken nodded his head. "I suspect Mona has all that already in hand and is planning to host the wedding. She's probably already set a date and blocked out the entire Inn for out-of-town-guests."

Ken reached across the seat and squeezed Abby's hand. "I have no idea what I would have done if you'd said no."

◈

On Christmas morning, Abby and Carmen watched out the front door glass as Ken pulled his truck to the curb in front of the Paper Box. Abby let them out of the store, and they bounded across the sidewalk and bounced up into the truck, Carmen in the back seat and Abby in front.

"Ladies," Ken said smiling.

"How are you, Ken?" Carmen asked from the back seat.

"Just swell, as usual," he replied. "Other than my mouth has been watering for the delicious meal waiting for us at the Inn."

"Merry Christmas and thanks for picking us up," Abby said to Ken. "We could have walked, but this way we don't have to bundle up so much."

A minute later Ken swung his truck around the circular drive at the Wander Inn, stopping directly in front of the front doors. "You two get out here," he instructed. "I'll park and see you inside."

Abby and Carmen entered and were instantly comforted by the warmth of the foyer. They were also instantly greeted by Mona, who was standing there giving last-minute instructions to the temporary servers who would help serve Christmas dinner to the hotel guests in the large dining room.

After dismissing the servers, Mona said very excitedly, "Hello, dear. I am so happy for you."

"I know!" Abby said. "Can you believe it? Want to see the ring?"

"Actually, I've already seen it, but yes, I'd love another look."

Abby held out her hand for Mona to admire the ring. "It is beautiful, dear, certainly befitting such a beautiful bride. I know last night was huge for you, and I promise we will circle back to it later. Right now, I feel like we should focus on Dennis and Elise."

Having praised Ken's taste in rings, which she credited to Marcus, Mona advised, "We'll be dining in the private dining room this year. The Inn is completely booked, and all the guests will be eating in the grand dining room. Except for Dennis, of course. I've instructed him to come down at three o'clock, and to go directly to the private room."

Abby glanced at her watch. "It's almost three now. Should we go ahead in there so Dennis won't be alone?"

Just then Ken entered the foyer, eliciting a polite smile from Mona. He waved and walked over to the group.

"Yes," Mona said. "Why don't you and Ken and Carmen go ahead in and keep Dennis company. Marcus and Elise will be here around three fifteen. When they get here, I'll escort them in."

With that Mona spun around and quickly vanished toward the kitchen. *I can't believe she didn't even acknowledge Carmen,* Abby thought. *Or maybe I can.*

Dennis appeared to have just arrived as Abby, Ken, and Carmen entered the private room. He was standing casually with his back to the wall opposite the only door, looking calm and relaxed, as was his way.

The foursome stood and made small talk for the next few minutes. Abby made sure to stand where she could see out the door and into the foyer. She caught her breath when she saw Marcus enter the foyer. Sure enough, Elise was by his side.

It's go time.

Abby watched as Mona greeted the brother and sister. Marcus took Mona's left hand, lifted it to his lips and kissed it. Mona even hugged Elise, and fake kissed her on the cheek. A server took their coats, and Abby took a deep breath as she watched Mona lead them toward the private dining room.

Mona entered first, then stood aside as Marcus and Elise came into the room. Abby thought Elise looked marvelous. She was wearing a long-sleeved navy-blue jersey knit dress, with two beautiful and colorful shawls, one draped around her shoulders, and one tied around her waist. Her ears were adorned with curious earrings that had a distinctive native American vibe. Her brown lace up knee length boots completed the look, and Abby thought, although she would never wear such an outfit, it looked almost prefect on Elise. When they were completely in, Mona began, "Welcome, all, to the Wander Inn. Merry Christmas, and we are delighted to have you as friends. I don't think introductions will be necessary, as I believe we all know each other."

Abby watched as Elise's eyes scanned the room. She watched as they landed on Dennis. She watched as they lit up with surprise. Elise gasped audibly, crossed her hands tightly to her chest, a joyful smile beginning to spread across her face.

"Dennis?!" she said, half a question, half a statement. "What …? How …?" she stuttered.

Abby turned to see Dennis's reaction. "Elise," he said, a look of pure joy overtaking his features. "Oh my gosh. It's been forever," he added in a soft, loving voice.

Abby noticed Elise's gaze shift from Dennis' face to the wall above. Dennis followed her gaze and turned to see what was capturing her attention so completely.

He said to Elise. "Those are your paintings. I mean, those are mine."

"Those are ours," Elise managed to say between jubilant sobs. "Oh, Dennis. Those are ours."

Dennis immediately hurried around the table and approached Elise. He enveloped her in a desperate embrace, as she sniffled and sobbed with happiness. He kissed her, and with the whole group staring in disbelief, he asked, "Can we please stop being stubborn old fools now?"

Elise laughed as she cried. "Of course. Let's stop being stubborn old fools."

By now, Abby, Carmen, and even Mona, were dabbing at the corners of their eyes, while Ken and Marcus were staring at their shoes.

Abby watched, her heart soaring higher than it had for a long time, as Dennis led Elise by the hand back around the table, pulled a chair out for her, and took a seat right beside her. *How happy they look!* Abby thought. *They're even holding hands.*

Soon the whole group was seated, and of course Abby made sure she sat beside Elise so she could eavesdrop. Telly came in with the champagne and filled everyone's flutes. Mona, seated in her usual place at the head of the table, toasted the occasion and received a loud return of "Hear, hear!"

Through a crack in the door between the dining room and kitchen, Abby saw Telly speaking with the servers and the temporary sous chef. She thought it odd that his hand was resting on a dining chair. She watched with curiosity as he picked up the chair, carried it into the private room, and walked over to where Carmen was sitting. He pointed to a bit of empty space beside her, and simply said, "May I?"

Carmen seemed surprised, then delighted. Her face lit up almost as bright as Elise's. "Of course," she said, scooching her chair over so his would fit at the table. "Please do."

Nobody spoke for a second, and Abby realized that this was probably the first time Telly had actually joined a formal gathering at the Inn. He was always the chef. The maître d'hôtel. Mona had told Abby that she had invited Telly to join her social gatherings many times, but he always refused. She had just stopped asking. But Abby got the impression that this afternoon, he had not been asked.

"Are you joining us for dinner?" Mona asked through pursed lips and with a strained voice.

"Should it please the proprietor, yes, I would be honored." *Wow, I've never heard Telly speak like that. Must be showing off for Carmen.*

"Very well. So, am I to assume the kitchen is squared away?" Mona asked tersely.

Telly simply smiled and nodded his head in the affirmative.

As the dinner progressed, Abby had her ear trained in Elise's direction, intent on gleaning every tidbit she could about how the reunion was going. At one point she overheard Dennis say to Elise, "I didn't think you ever came to these Christmas dinners."

"I came sometimes. But not very often. I guess it would have been better for me to get out more. Marcus insisted I come tonight," she explained.

 "I think this reunion was a setup," Dennis revealed.

"Well, whoever set us up, I am extremely grateful," said Elise.

"So am I," Dennis agreed. "So am I. And I think that wonderful lady sitting beside you might have had something to do with it.'

Elise turned to Abby, not knowing that Abby had just over-heard every word of their conversation. Abby was pretending to be listening to a conversation between Marcus and Ken when Elise said, "Abby, if you had anything to do with bringing Dennis back to Wander Creek, thank you from the bottom of my heart."

"Oh, Elise," Abby said. "You don't have to thank me. I don't know, getting you two back together, or at least giving it a chance to happen, sort of became a mission for me."

"But, why?" Elise asked. Now the rest of the table was listening to Abby and Elise. "I know you know Dennis from Pages bookstore, but you barely know me at all."

"Honestly, Elise, it was those paintings. When Marcus told me you had painted them, and that they were of Dennis, and of the circumstances—I simply could not get them out of my mind. And of course, I couldn't get you and Dennis out of my mind," Abby explained.

Every head turned toward the paintings. "You remember painting them?" Dennis asked Elise.

"Of course, I do. I remember we would take the train from Paris down to Rambouillet. Remember? We would have lunch at an outdoor café and stroll to the outskirts of town where the farms and meadows began. We would have wine, and you would read. And I would paint."

Dennis smiled, closed his eyes, and sat silent for at least a minute. When he opened his eyes, all he said was, "Like it was yesterday, my love."

"So how did those paintings end up here, in a private dining room at the Wander Inn?" Elise asked the table.

Before Abby could say anything, Mona declared, "We have Abby Barrett to thank for that."

"Well, me sort of. More like me and Ken together," Abby said. "You see, after I bought Pages and decided to turn it into the Book Box, I wanted to spruce the place up a little bit. Not that it needed it, Dennis. You understand. Anyway, one of the plaster walls had a lot of cracks in it, so I got Ken to pull out the old plaster and replace it with drywall. He found the paintings in the wall. They had been placed inside the wall, and then plastered over."

Elise turned to face Dennis. "Well?" she said.

"I had pretty much forgotten about those paintings," Dennis said. "Probably more like forced myself to forget about them. You remember right after you decided we were just not going to work out, I was heartbroken. I brought those paintings back to the States with me. They were my only physical connection to you. They were the only things I owned that had actually been touched by your hands. But losing you was so hard on me. I couldn't keep the paintings. But I couldn't get rid of them. So, one weekend I entombed them in that wall. That's probably why Abby had to replace the wall. I was not a good plasterer. Anyway, with them in that wall, I would always know where they were. I would always know they were mine, and that they were safe. In a weird way, protecting those paintings in that wall was my way of protecting you. Having them in that wall meant I couldn't take them out every five minutes and mourn the loss of us. I know, it seems crazy, but I was so in love with you, and it just hurt."

"I'm glad you hid them," Elise said, her face beaming with joy.

Abby continued the story. "So, I showed the paintings to Marcus and Mona one evening at my apartment, and when Marcus saw them, he looked like he had seen a ghost."

"I hadn't seen those paintings for thirty years either," Marcus said. "I had visited Elise in Paris when she and Dennis were madly in love, and she had shown them to me. She asked me if I thought they were good enough to give Dennis," Marcus explained.

"And you said they were good enough for the Louvre," said Elise.

"I don't remember," Marcus admitted. "But I do remember they had a profound effect on me. I thought they were wonderful. I memorized them. I could pull them up in my mind's eye at will. That's why I was so shocked when Abby showed them to me."

The conversation drifted away from the paintings and to how Elise and Dennis met and what they used to be like as a couple. Neither of them mentioned their estrangement. Abby thought it was as if they had never broken up.

Mona made sure that everyone knew about Marcus' proposal to her, and about Ken's proposal to Abby. "Abby, care to tell us about how you were proposed to?" Mona teased.

Abby was more than happy to tell the story of how Jessica had tricked her into riding along on an emergency grocery store trip for Honeycrisp apples to Two Harbors, only to find a jewelry box in the apple display, a handsome man named Ken dressed in a blue pin-striped suit approaching her, a crazy lady named Jessica recording it all on her phone, and a whole store of grocery customers cheering and hollering as Ken asked Abby to make him the happiest man in the world. "Of course, I said yes," she said.

"Did you suspect anything, dear? Mona asked.

"Well, I've never known you to have a grocery emergency. And Jessica said that you had twisted her arm to drive to Two Harbors because Telly really needed them for today. Total load of bull." The whole table laughed.

Abby, overjoyed at all the goodwill and love and Christmas cheer packed into that small private dining room, smiled from ear to ear.

CHAPTER 15

*A*s Abby opened the Paper Box the morning after Christmas, she was surprised to see that Naomi's shop was still dark. She kept an eye on the building throughout the day but was so busy with the after-Christmas sale that she almost missed the unmarked moving truck that pulled up in front of Naomi's store. Two men and two women got out of the truck and went into the dark building.

Naomi must already be in there, she thought. *And if it's going to take four people to unload that truck that means she's bought a lot of new stock.*

The days after Christmas proceeded smoothy, and Abby was glad for a lull in customers, giving her a chance to catch her breath. Emma seamlessly moved between the three stores, helping with customers, restocking, and spelling Abby, Carmen, and Jessica for lunch breaks. Thing were going so well, in fact, that Abby thought they might want to bring on another full-time person to work on marketing in addition to being a sales associate. Business would pick up in February when ice fishing season began.

Whenever Emma relieved Abby, she headed over to the Book

Box, pausing momentarily on the sidewalk to glance at Naomi's store. She couldn't help herself. That day, Abby was surprised to see that the movers were not bringing boxes into the building, they were bringing boxes, furniture, and display stands *out* of the building and placing them into the truck.

Naomi emerged from the store and ran across the street. "Are you happy now Abby Barrett? You've run me out of business."

Abby laughed. "I think you did that yourself, Naomi, selling your inventory at a huge loss and even giving away books. That was never going to work."

"Nevertheless, I expect you to buy some of my stock," Naomi said officiously. "There are a bunch of boxes of stationery items and books in the shop. You can have it all for two thousand dollars."

Stunned, Abby wasn't sure how to respond. Then she put her thumbs in her ears, wiggled her fingers, and sang two verses of "na-na, na-na, boo-boo," and left a shocked Naomi staring after her as she stepped into the Book Box, laughing so hard she thought she might split a seam. She couldn't wait to tell Carmen.

≈

"Are you as exhausted as I am?" Abby asked Mona as she accepted a glass of wine and tucked her shoeless feet under her on Mona's chintz couch. The Paper Box and Book Box were closed and shuttered for the night, and Abby was happy to be ensconced in Mona's cozy apartment with a fire blazing. They could hear the low murmur of the Inn guests enjoying themselves in the parlors or going up the stairs to their rooms.

"I should be but I'm not," Mona said. "I think I am running on adrenaline and happiness. Let me see your ring again."

Abby held her hand up and watched the diamond catch the light. "I've never thanked you for the part you played in the proposal. It was really very special."

Mona held Abby's fingers and observed the ring. "Ken found the perfect ring and it looks gorgeous on you."

Abby took back her hand, gazing down at the ring.

"I'm just going to throw something out and you tell me if I'm wrong or if I'm right, or if you don't want to talk about it. Here goes. You don't seem terribly happy for a woman who has recently become engaged. To an awesome catch, I might add. You haven't said a peep about wedding plans or a dress or anything."

Abby sighed. "I hope it's not that obvious to anyone else, especially not to Ken."

"Don't worry about him, you said yes and that's all that matters for now. But what's going on?" Mona asked, a look of genuine concern on her face.

"We only got engaged three days ago," Abby pointed out.

"Yes, but you've been here for almost a half hour and haven't mentioned the subject once. I had to bring it up when I asked to see your ring," Mona pointed out.

"Okay. Here's the thing. I'm gun shy about getting married again. I love Ken and want to spend my life with him, but after seeing my first marriage implode and my life go into a tailspin, well, I guess I'm just hesitant about sharing my life with someone in a legal way," Abby revealed.

"Oh honey, Ken would never do anything to hurt you. He adores you."

"That's what I thought about Jake, too, and look how that turned out," Abby said.

Mona took Abby's hand again and squeezed it. "You can't go through life scared of what might happen. You will miss out on so much if you do. And you'll never know what you're missing if you don't take chances."

"I know," Abby conceded. "I have a lot of thinking to do. And I owe it to Ken to be honest with him. The last thing I want to do is hurt him."

"If you're honest and he knows how much you love him, then you won't. Do you want to talk about it some more?"

Abby shook her head and Mona changed the subject.

"I ran into Naomi the other day. Did you know that she's going out of business and has to sell her building to pay the mortgages on the other properties she purchased?" Mona asked.

Abby then described her last encounter with her nemesis. That woman did not have a head for business.

"I probably shouldn't tell you this but I'm going to because it's too good not to. Naomi gleefully revealed to me what the initials of her company names stand for," said Mona.

"Oh yeah?"

"Yes, and get this. IHAB Ltd., stands for 'I hate Abby Barrett,' and IWGY stands for 'I Will Get You.' That woman sure can carry a grudge."

"That is really creepy. You don't think she's dangerous, do you?" Abby asked, a look of genuine concern on her face.

"I don't think so. Besides, she'll be gone shortly. She's going to have to sell all her properties if she's going to come out of this whole mess with any money at all."

"How do you know all this?" Abby asked. Then she said, "Forget it. I don't think I want to know."

"Don't be silly. I have a good friend in Duluth who is a realtor, and she just happens to be helping Naomi with the sales."

"Lucky her," Abby said. "Now can we please talk about something else?"

"Yes, indeed," Mona declared, "let's talk about setting a date for your wedding."

"I was thinking more along the lines of Telly and Carmen," Abby said.

"Oh? And what about them?"

"You know perfectly well what I mean. They're getting closer.

Nothing says that more than when he joined the Christmas dinner. I almost fell out of my chair when he did that. And you should have seen the look on your face. I wish I could have taken a picture. Your mouth was practically hanging open."

"It was not," Mona said hotly. "I would never do such an uncouth thing and you know that."

"You have to give up this childish battle between you and Carmen," Abby said pleadingly. "And you should be happy for Telly that he found someone to love. People are not meant to be alone."

Mona sighed and agreed begrudgingly. "Okay, I will try to do better. How about I invite Telly and Carmen out to dinner at the Bistro one evening? Or better yet, I'll have them here and cook a meal myself. I know how to cook four things. Maybe you can help me."

"I am almost afraid to ask what meals you know how to make," Abby said.

"Hard-boiled eggs. The secret is to let them sit in the hot water for twelve minutes after turning off the flame. I also can make an omelet, brownies, and cranberry sauce with orange juice and candied ginger."

"An interesting combination," Abby observed. "And you're right, I can help you. In fact, I think I owe it to Carmen and Telly to help you. Now let's talk about *your* wedding. Have you set a date? What do you have in mind?"

Mona grinned. "All you need to know is to show up here January eighth at eleven in the morning. Wear a pretty dress and bring Ken."

"You're getting married in a week?" Abby asked, aghast.

Mona patted Abby's hand. "At my age, dear, I can't afford to wait."

~

As Abby walked back to the Paper Box from Mona's she noticed the soft yellow lights aglow in the Book Box. Carmen often worked late, and Abby decided it was time. She couldn't shake the feeling that Carmen had not really settled into her new role at the Book Box. Tomorrow night Abby would finally talk to Carmen.

Carmen was always pleasant and positive when they spoke about the shop, but there wasn't the enthusiasm Carmen demonstrated for her own store in Minneapolis. At the Paperie, where Abby had worked for a year after her life fell apart, Carmen practically buzzed with positive energy. She went bonkers when she found new and interesting stock to order, and she was ecstatic when it came to decorating for Christmas. And she had a special place in her heart for the fresh and lovely brides-to-be who came to the Paperie for wedding invitations all throughout the year.

Abby had to find out what was wrong, for both their sakes. It had been almost two months since Carmen came to Wander Creek and took over as manager. It was time to take the temperature of the room. After their stores closed, Abby surprised Carmen at the Book Box with a bottle of wine and a picnic basket laden with yummy appetizers.

"Uh, oh," Carmen said, when Abby came into to shop right after closing time. "Beware of people bearing gifts. Or whatever the saying is."

"That's for strangers," Abby said. "And you are my dear friend. I come with comfort food and wine, the nectar of life, plus I have an open heart."

The two sat in Carmen's office and Abby arranged a plate of cheeses and crackers and another plate containing figs, grapes, and apple slices."

"Pretty sure I know what this is about," Carmen said,

spreading thick and creamy Brie on a cracker and popping it into her mouth.

Abby noticed that as usual, Carmen was impeccably dressed in a wool suit and silk scarf, just as she had always been at her store in Minneapolis, which was located in the heart of a very fancy and upscale shopping district. Why hadn't she noticed before that Carmen was still dressing for Minneapolis shoppers, instead of the lower-key clientele that came to Wander Creek? That should have been a clue to where Carmen's heart and mind were.

"If you already know then that makes this easier for me," Abby said.

"I'll make it easier for you, and not beat around the bush," Carmen responded. "I can't stay in Wander Creek any longer. I miss the city so badly. I miss Minneapolis. I think I knew within the first few weeks that I needed to go back home, but I didn't want to let you down or make you angry. And I would never have left until after the grand opening and until we had made it through Christmas. I hope you know that."

"I could never be angry at you, Carmen," Abby said. "We both knew that you coming here was on a trial basis. I will be incredibly sad to see you go. I'm sure Telly will be, too."

Carmen sighed. "It's hard to leave him," she admitted. "We've only known each other for a few weeks, but I feel a connection to him that I've not felt for anyone since my husband died all those years ago."

"Have you told him yet?" Abby asked gently.

Carmen nodded. "He came over last night for dinner and we had a wonderful talk. We care about each other but neither of us is willing to give up our lifestyles to be together. That sounds so selfish of us, doesn't it?"

"I disagree," Abby assured her. "On the contrary, I think it's selfless. Think what a mess there would be if you stayed here and continued to miss the city and grew miserable and resentful. Or if Telly moved to Minneapolis, to a faster pace of life he isn't used to. And far away from Mona and the job he loves. The two of you would end up resenting each other."

Carmen nodded her head. "You're right, of course. I just wish things could have turned out differently. But Telly wouldn't be Telly if he wasn't devoted to his job and to Mona. And I wouldn't be me without the vibrancy of the city around me. Museums, concerts, art galleries. I need all that at my fingertips."

"Does this have anything to do with Mona?" Abby asked.

Carmen laughed. "Not at all. It's true that we were never going to be the best of friends. The best of enemies, maybe. But no. If I were to stay here Mona and I would either work things out or continue to swap barbs at social gatherings. It must be fun to watch us try and one up each other."

"Fun isn't the word I would have chosen," Abby laughed, then grew serious. "When do you plan on going?"

"I need to start the New Year in my condo in Minneapolis, looking over the lights of downtown, having dinner at a neighborhood restaurant, watching the Times Square ball on my television when it falls. Now before you start worrying, I have it all worked out for you. Emma can take over the manager position at the Book Box. And you said that there were a few of the candidates that you interviewed for Emma's job that you liked. Get one of them lined up. I wouldn't leave you in a lurch. And I wouldn't leave you if I didn't think you could handle this hurdle." She put her hand on Abby's cheek. "You are my protégé and it's been such an honor to see you bloom and develop into the confident and successful woman you are."

Abby raised her wine glass. "A toast then, to successful women and following our hearts."

Carmen left the day before New Year's Eve. It was a bittersweet parting. Abby had loved having Carmen around, but on the other hand, she was looking forward to putting Emma in charge of the Book Box. Emma had accepted the manager job on the spot and had stepped into the role effortlessly. She was bursting with ideas for moving the shop forward and even making it a destination attraction for shoppers from around the region. Emma even planned to visit the bookstore in Duluth, their nearest competitor, to scope out the competition.

Abby realized that life was always a series of choices between moving backwards, standing still, or moving forward. And each person had to make those choices for themselves. Emma wanted to move forward by leaps and bounds. Abby didn't blame Carmen for wanting to go back to the life she loved in Minneapolis. If that's what made sense for her, then she needed to follow her gut.

We all do, Abby thought.

CHAPTER 16

*K*en let himself in the front door of the Paper Box and practically ran up the stairs. When he abruptly appeared in Abby's living room, he found himself alone.

Abby had obviously heard him come in. "I'll be right out. Just give me a sec. Aren't you early?" she called from the bedroom.

"I don't think so," he replied. "It's eight on the dot. Want me to go downstairs and wait?" he joked.

Just then Abby made her grand entrance.

"Happy New Year!" she exclaimed.

"Wow! Look at you," Ken responded. "You look awesome."

"Thank you," she said, smiling happily. She was wearing a smart sleeveless black sheath dress that fit her perfectly. Her ears were adorned with shiny red and green and gold earrings that were actually made from tiny fishing lures, a nod to Ken's business. She decided not to put up her honey-blonde hair as was her usual formal style, and it hung gracefully down past her shoulders, tucked behind her ears.

"I mean it," Ken repeated. "You look awesome."

"Keep it up and I'll get embarrassed," Abby warned playfully, basking in the warmth of Ken's approval. "You don't look so bad yourself, mister."

"Well, I couldn't show up to New Year's Eve dinner with the girl of my dreams dressed like a hobo, now could I?" They both laughed, and Ken stepped closer and hugged Abby, giving her a loving peck on the cheek. "You smell good, too."

Abby then headed into the kitchen, calling over her shoulder, "I made one of your favorites."

"I know. I could smell it when I came in. You make the best chicken cacciatore I've ever had," Ken said.

"The table is set," Abby announced. "Go ahead and have a seat and I'll serve."

A few minutes later she placed her signature dish in the middle of the farmhouse style table, then returned to the kitchen to remove the garlic toast from the oven. She placed the bread on a large tray already bearing two beautiful salads stacked with crisp greens, sliced vegetables and fruits, a smattering of pumpkin seeds, and drizzled with Abby's own blackberry balsamic vinaigrette dressing. After everything was placed, Abby settled in the chair across from Ken with a contented sigh.

She raised her water glass and said, "Shall we have a toast?"

"With water?" Ken asked. "Want me to pour us some wine? I've heard that it's really bad luck to toast with water."

"Really?" Abby asked, knowing she was going to check this on the internet as soon as she got the chance.

"Absolutely," Ken assured her. "Toasting with water brings bad luck. Even death. All the military manuals forbid it. Hang on, I'll get us some wine."

After pouring them each a glass, Ken retook his seat opposite Abby.

"I had no idea you were so superstitious," she said.

"Well, you know, I'm really not. It's just I've always been told you gotta have wine, beer, champagne or something. Otherwise, you know …" Ken wrenched his mouth into a grotesque shape and slashed an imaginary knife across his throat, causing Abby to laugh loudly.

"Okay, a toast," Ken said raising his glass. "You gonna do it or you want me to?"

"I'll do it," said Abby, gathering her thoughts. "To us. To us in the New Year. To who we are, and who we'll become. Both individually, and as a couple."

Abby couldn't swear to it, but she thought she saw a little bit of watering in Ken's eyes. "Hear, hear!," he said, enthusiastically.

The meal progressed pleasantly, with neither of them shy about piling the delicious cacciatore upon their plates and sopping up the left-over sauce with garlic toast. When the table had been cleared and the dishes placed in the dishwasher, the couple retired to Abby's couch in front of the television to watch a movie.

"What do you want to watch?" Abby asked.

"I don't care, as long as it has action, guns, chase scenes, and explosions," Ken said, knowing this was absolutely not an option.

"I was thinking something more, I don't know, more ..."

"Don't say it!" Ken warned loudly.

But Abby ignored him, and said just as loudly, "More romantic."

"Oh my gosh. I can't believe you said it. Now I'm going to have to leave," he said playfully, standing as if he really meant it.

"Sit down," Abby commanded, and Ken obeyed. "I've decided we are going to watch *Sleepless in Seattle.*"

"Okay," Ken said compliantly. "But I cannot be held responsible for any comments I might make during the movie."

Abby and Ken watched the movie, and as Abby knew would happen, Ken loved it just as much as she did. The only problem was that Abby's phone kept buzzing, but she just ignored it. When the movie ended, she looked down and saw that Mona had texted her multiple times. First, there was, "Abby, this is Mona.

Please call me on my cell phone. You have the number." Then came a text with just two question marks. And the final text read, "ABBY, THIS IS MONA AGAIN. EMERGENCY, CALL NOW."

Knowing Mona, Abby did not panic at the word "emergency." She glanced at Ken, stood up and asked, "Do you mind if I call her real quick?'

"Only if you put her on speaker," Ken joked.

Abby tapped Mona's number. She answered before the first ring was over. "Guess what happened to me tonight?" Mona practically shouted.

"I'm sure I have no idea," Abby responded. "Was it good or bad?"

"Good, my dear. Very good! Marcus proposed to me."

Abby knew they were getting closer as a couple, but marriage? "And what did you say?" Abby asked.

"Don't be a dolt, dear," Mona replied smartly. "Yes! I said yes, of course."

"Well, Ken and I are very happy for you ..." Abby was saying when Mona interrupted.

"Sorry dear, I must go. Marcus has just uncorked another bottle. Happy New Year!" With that, Mona abruptly ended the call, leaving Abby staring at the phone in her hand.

She told Ken, "Marcus just proposed to Mona tonight."

"I gathered," Ken said. "I figured it might happen. Just didn't think it would be this soon."

Abby sank back onto the couch. "I wonder when they are going to get married?" she asked, knowing instantly that that question also applied to her and Ken.

Sure enough, Ken said, "I wonder the same thing about us."

Abby remained quiet for a moment, then leaned over against Ken's shoulder and began to speak. "Well, about that. I know you're anxious, or at least my sense is that you are, for us to tie the knot."

"The sooner the better for me," Ken said, a big, happy smile upon his face.

"Ken, I was really hoping we could have a long engagement. Here me out. My first marriage ended in disaster. I know I told you about it, but I'm not sure I ever made it clear how difficult it was for me. My whole life was ripped out from under me. Everything I valued, or thought I valued, was yanked from my grip. I pretty much felt utterly destroyed. And it really wasn't that long ago. Just a few years. I'm getting over it, getting my confidence back, and I do want to be your wife, and I don't want any man besides you—it's just that, I guess I'm scared."

"What are you scared of?" Ken asked softly, squeezing her hand.

"Lots of things. Everything. Not being able to be a good wife for you—the wife you deserve. Not being able to hold myself together as an entrepreneur and losing everything. Getting divorced and losing my shirt. Again. Being kidnapped and eaten by Naomi. The list is pretty long," Abby confessed.

"Are you sure you're not just building in an escape hatch?" Ken asked.

"What do you mean?" asked Abby.

"I mean, it seems like you need more time to deal with stuff before we get married. How do I know more time won't lead to more and more time, and before you know it you take back your 'yes'?"

"Oh, Ken," Abby said sympathetically. "I know it's not fair to you for me to be like this. But I promise you, I want to marry you. I will never take back my 'yes'. I swear it."

"I believe you," Ken said, wrapping his arm around her shoulder.

The couple sat silently for a minute or two, and then Abby said, "Oh, I almost forgot. There's something I need to ask you."

"I'm not sure I like the sound of that," Ken replied.

Abby laughed. "No, it's nothing bad. Do you remember Mona's birthday party?"

Ken raised his eyebrows. "Of course. Why, did I do something stupid?"

"No," Abby said. "It's just I caught a glimpse of you and Marcus looking at something. It looked like a jewelry box."

"Ohhhh," Ken said, drawing it out dramatically. "A jewelry box, huh?"

"Is that what it was?"

"Maybe," Ken teased.

"Come on. Tell me," Abby pleaded.

"Yes, it was a jewelry box. I'm not an expert on women's jewelry, and so I thought a sophisticated guy like Marcus might be able to make sure I hadn't purchased something awful."

"So, you were showing my ring to Marcus?" she asked, relieved to get clarification.

"Sure. Whose ring did you think it was?" Ken asked.

"I wasn't sure. I wasn't even sure it was an engagement ring. If it was, I thought it could go either way. I knew Marcus was pretty sweet on Mona. But I guess I thought it more likely it was my ring."

Ken took Abby's left hand and held it up between them, admiring the ring, touching it with his thumb. "Yep, it was yours all the time. I was just waiting for the right time to give it to you. Or at least offer it to you. I gotta tell you I was more than a little relieved when you accepted."

Just then the alarm on Abby's phone sounded. "Oh my gosh," she said. "It's almost midnight. New Year's is in five minutes!"

"Not to worry, my dear," Ken was saying as he stepped into the kitchen. He was watching the digital clock on the microwave as he removed a champagne bottle from the fridge, expertly popped the cork, and poured them each a glass. Abby joined him and he handed her a champagne flute. They stood facing each other as the clock ticked down. At exactly midnight, Ken raised his glass. Abby did the same. When the clock read midnight, they each took a sip of champagne.

"Happy New Year!" Abby exclaimed. And then, in a fervent tone, she said, "I love you, Ken."

"I love you too," he responded. "Into the New Year and every year after."

CHAPTER 17

*W*hen Abby awoke on New Year's Day it was with a full heart and so many good memories of recent days, and she felt like her brain might burst with ideas and plans for the future. She and Jessica had gone ahead and hired another salesclerk to replace Emma, and she was scheduled to start the following week. Things were falling back into place.

Emma had agreed to spend the day with Abby at the Book Box so Abby could bring her completely up to speed on the management aspects of the store. Abby wasn't worried in the least. Emma was a quick learner and incredibly smart. Plus, anyone that could put Naomi Dale in her place could do just about anything in Abby's book.

And then there was Mona. Dear Mona, always full of contradictions and surprises. Diamonds and chicken wings. A larger-than-life personality but a small apartment in a smallish inn practically in the middle of nowhere. *Definitely in the middle of nowhere.*

In the first week of the new year, Mona surprised Abby, and probably the entire town of Wander Creek, by completely organizing her and Marcus' wedding. And in less than a week. There would be no ice sculptures, orchids flown in from Brazil, or hand-blown and monogrammed champagne flutes. No somme-lier, no soloist or band, no elaborate decorations. Instead, Mona and Marcus would get married in one of the Wander Inn parlors with just a few of their favorite people as witnesses. The Wander Creek mayor had been delighted when asked to serve as officiant, perhaps thinking it might lead to a few votes come next election day.

Mona chose a cream Chanel suit from her closet declaring it, "What, this old thing?"

Unfortunately, the wedding coordination came together so quickly that Mona's son Ian would not be able to attend, but that did not seem to bother Mona.

A week to the day from when Marcus proposed, Ken, Abby, Telly, Jessica and her son Aiden joined Marcus and the mayor in a private parlor on the Inn's first floor just off the foyer. Mona's absence was glaring. And it grew more uncomfortable with each passing minute that Mona did not appear. Marcus did not look the least bit worried, but Abby was. Mona was a stickler for punctuality. Being late to someone's wedding was positively gauche. Being late to your own wedding would be unthinkable.

Abby squeezed Ken's hand. "I better go see what's going on," she whispered.

He nodded and Abby slipped out of the parlor and rushed down the hallway to Mona's apartment, knocking softly, then letting herself in. She found Mona sitting on the bed worrying a tissue in her lap. Abby could tell that she had been crying. Some-how, though, her make-up remained impeccable.

Abby sat down next to her friend and saw that they were looking at their reflections in the large mirror hanging on the wall. Abby put her arm around Mona's shoulders and said gently, "What's going on?"

Mona dabbed at her eyes. "Look at me," she said, gesturing at the mirror. "A seventy-something woman behaving like a silly girl. Getting married. At my age. It's humiliating. What must people think of me? And now I've only made it worse by being late to my own wedding."

"Since when do you care about what other people think of you? Everyone loves and respects you and we all want to see you happy." Abby caught Mona's gaze in the mirror. "And all I see in the mirror is my beautiful, vibrant friend who has taught me so much about life and how it should be lived."

"I have?" Mona hiccuped, but she didn't let Abby answer. "Then there's the Inn and where we will live. We haven't talked any of that through. This is so impulsive. It borders on crazy."

"You will work it all out. Marcus adores you and will support you in anything you want to do. And as far as the Inn goes, from what I can tell you have such an amazing staff that it practically runs itself."

Mona patted Abby's arm. "You're right, of course. I am too strong a person to worry about all these details. But what am I going to tell Marcus about being late? He must hate me."

"You let me take care of that. Take a deep breath, have a glass of water and come out when you're ready. But make it soon, okay?"

Mona laughed and nodded.

When Abby returned to the parlor she went directly to Marcus, who still waited patiently at the front of the room, expecting his bride to arrive any minute.

Abby whispered in Marcus' ear, "One of Mona's necklaces got caught in the tag of her suit jacket. And the more she pulled, the worse it got. I got it untangled and she'll be here any minute."

Marcus let out a sigh of relief and Abby realized he had been more worried than he let on. Poor Marcus. He was going to have his hands full with his wonderful, spirited, and irrepressible wife.

Just as Abby took her seat next to Ken and whispered, "It's under control," Mona appeared in the doorway, holding a single long-stemmed white rose that Abby guessed Marcus had given her.

Mona took her place next to Marcus and grasped his hand. Telly leaned over from where he sat, and Mona handed him the rose. That was Telly, still and always taking care of Mona. *Marcus will just have to get used to that.*

Following the vows there were tears and laughter, toasts, and funny stories about Mona and Marcus. It was all deliciously cozy and somehow, despite Mona's grand personality, just right.

Dennis and Elise were sitting close together on a loveseat looking so happy they practically shone. Like Marcus and Mona, they would have to work out logistical details and decide what shape their lives would take. Each would have to compromise and give up something. Abby thought of the gazebo that Elise decorated each year, and the paintings that Dennis hid because they were too painful to look at. So much time had passed. Was it wasted time? Or did that much time have to pass before the two of them could be happy together? Abby glanced at Telly who was re-filling Mona's champagne. Did he miss Carmen?

Abby looked across the room to where Ken was talking with Jessica and her little boy. They were all smiling and laughing. Was Abby wasting time, too, by worrying about what-ifs and things that hadn't yet happened? She and Ken also would have to work out where they would live, too. Would they have children? They'd never discussed it. But if marriage wasn't a leap of faith, she didn't know what was. With a smile on her face and a fluttering heart, Abby walked across the room, and slipped her hand into Ken's.

THE END

AMY RUTH ALLEN

$\mathcal{I}$f you enjoyed this book, please leave a review/rating and follow me on Facebook and Goodreads. Thank you.

ABOUT THE AUTHOR

Amy Ruth Allen writes wholesome, uplifting women's fiction that celebrates the power of friendship, love and self-discovery, the charms of small town life, and the joy of a life well-lived. Lose yourself in her two feel-good series, Wander Creek and Finch's Crossing. Stay in touch by joining her newsletter at amyruthallen.com/newsletter. Amy lives in Minneapolis, Minnesota with her husband and their rescue pup Jessica Fletcher.

For Leigh, always.

ALSO BY AMY RUTH ALLEN

FINCH'S CROSSING SERIES

Finch's Crossing is a heartwarming series following the lives of the four Hamilton sisters as they search for love, personal fulfillment, and a renewed connection to the place they call home. Each Finch's Crossing book evokes the special joys of the seasons and the charms of small town life. Fans of Debbie Macomber's Cedar Cove series will be happily drawn into the life of this beloved community. To read excerpts and reviews, and learn more about the real town that inspired the Finch's Crossing series, visit amyruthallen.com.

Autumn (Book One)

How could she let this happen?

Autumn's life used to be idyllic. Now she may have to leave her happy life and lovely home in Finch's Crossing to save her career.

And here she is, with her own life in turmoil, standing in a pumpkin patch trying to save a little girl. The orphan is supposed to be moving with her new guardian to New York City.

Autumn may escalate things by trashing his car. He may call her a pumpkin bumpkin.

And she tells him in no-uncertain terms that he is obviously out of his league.

Autumn can't stand by and do nothing. It's in her nature to fix things. *She won't give up, and she's soon to find out, he will never back down.*

While she schemes to make things right, she's also battling a secret shame. Is it the reason why it's been so long since she's let a man into her life?

Gradually, he shows Autumn that he isn't a bad guy after all, and they can no longer deny the mutual attraction that has been building for months.

But a cruel revelation on Christmas Day changes everything.

Now what? Are they friends or enemies? Feelings don't just disappear overnight . . .

∾

Spring (Book Two)

Is this a second chance, or a second mistake?

Spring expects to see beautiful yellow and pink tulips blooming when she arrives in Finch's Crossing.

But she does not expect to see him. The man who broke her heart twenty years earlier.

And has he named his little bookshop after her? *Really?*

How dare he even try to talk to her!

She has only come for a quick visit with her sister. After all, she has an exciting future in New York City where she will be feted as one of the country's top models.

But the heart wants what the heart wants and they cannot resist the pull of the past.

Until his explosive secret past catches up with him. And catches her by surprise.

Is it time to pack her suitcases, *or should she give him another chance?*

∾

Summer (Book Three)

His timing couldn't be worse . . .

Summer has returned to Finch's Crossing to put down roots for the first time in a decade. She has a vibrant new business. A lovely childhood home full of happy memories. Good friends.

And *now* he comes into her life? This wonderful, wandering man.

Picnics. A shared interest in nature and well-being. Surprise gifts. *He loves her. She has found her soulmate.*

So his abrupt departure is as unexpected as it is painful.

What happened to the kind, genuine and nurturing man she has fallen in love with?

And why does she hear another woman in the background when they speak on the phone?

Is it time to let go, or time to make a grand gesture?

When the truth finally comes out, will she give him the chance to explain, or wonder forever what happened to their love?

Winter (Book Four)

When the mean girl meets her match . . .

Winter blows into Finch's Crossing with a broken leg. Taking over her lovely childhood home. Imposing on her sister. Alienating everyone around her.

Watching her perfect life in the city slip away one unanswered email at a time.

She knows she is bossy, selfish, ruthless and cold-hearted. It's how she climbed the corporate ladder and became a millionaire.

So it's hard to fathom that he sees beyond her icy demeanor to what's really in her heart. Pain. Regrets. Sadness.

As they grow closer, profound and dangerous circumstances lead Winter to do the unexpected.

Is it enough to make people like her? *When all is said and done, will the kindest man she's ever known become her champion?*

Then his kind nature leads him far, far away from her.

There is no ways she can go with him. Her leg has healed, but is her heart big enough now to make a sacrifice so they can be together? *She's not the only one who doesn't think so . . .*

WANDER CREEK SERIES

If you love wholesome women's fiction that celebrates friendship, second chances and the joys of a life well-lived, all against the backdrop of small-town living, you will fall in love with the Wander Creek series.

∿

A Place to Start (Book One)

What does she have to lose? She's already lost everything . . . literally.

Abby is still reeling from her husband's bombshell. Overnight, she went from rich and carefree socialite to social pariah.

She needs to lay low and out of the spotlight. A small town she's never heard of is as good a place as any. *But should she take the outrageous opportunity offered by an anonymous benefactor?*

Why not? She can't sink any lower.

He is her first friend in Wander Creek, but another woman has her hooks in him and many more want to paddle his canoe.

But he's taken a shy shining to her. He helps her set up her business and literally takes her on her first walk across a frozen lake. *And that sunrise ATV ride along Wander Creek . . .*

But then there's that snow bunny and Abby's public humiliation. *How could he do that to her?*

So what's the point in staying in Wander Creek? According to her crazy arrangement, she can leave after a year with the money. A lot of money.

She'll have to muster all the sass and moxie she can to decide whether to stay or go. Or is it possible that she can she do both?

When Abby's humiliating past is revealed another secret comes to the surface and shocks Abby to the core.

All of a sudden, his betrayal is the least of her worries . . .

∿

A Place to Stay (Book Two)

What happened to all the reasons she had to stay?

Abby runs a successful business in Wander Creek and has wonderful friends, including the irrepressible owner of the Wander Inn on the shores of the creek. *Abby could stay here forever.*

And the man in her life is kind, loving, and adventurous. A real man's man.

But then he sees something he wasn't supposed to see. She tries to explain, but his taillights are the last thing she sees of him for some time.

And the mean girl is back and determined to chase Abby out of Wander Creek. *The trouble is the law is not on Abby's side.*

But Abby isn't about to back down from a challenge. Especially since the mean girl has her sights set on Abby's beau. *Or is it ex-beau?*

Meanwhile, Abby finds herself in the middle of a magical mystery. But a dangerous situation makes Abby re-evaluate her life. Life is too precious to waste in arguments with people you love. But can Abby persuade her beau to give her a second chance?

Probably. Hopefully.

But then Abby sees something she wasn't supposed to see . . .

A Place for Christmas (Book Three)

What's a little spying and breaking and entering between frenemies?

Abby has gone from disgraced socialite and social pariah to successful entrepreneur and civic leader with a steady and comfortable love interest.

Christmas would be a romantic time to propose. If only Abby was certain she wanted him to.

Wait. Was there an engagement ring in the small velvet box she wasn't supposed to see? How did things get so muddled?

Christmastime in Wander Creek is magical, with the small hamlet decorated to the nines under a snowy blanket. Abby plans to enjoy every cozy moment at her stationery store, the Paper Box, and her new venture, the Book Box. Her nemesis has left town in disgrace and all seems peaceful in the quaint town. Until. . .

But old ghosts appear, Abby's own version of the Ghost of Christmas

Past, and things get out of control. What's a little spying and breaking and entering between frenemies?

Will the Ghost of Christmas Past ruin the new life she built for herself?

❧

Readers **LOVE** Wander Creek!

"**I absolutely loved this book.** I enjoyed all the characters, the good ones, bad ones, and crazy ones. The descriptive environment is wonderful, from her shabby apartment to her adventurous walks and rides around Wander Creek. **The story pulled me in** and I joined Abby on her decisions, friendships, goals and new love...maybe. What will Abby's future hold? Will her decisions help her for the better? Will all end up during spring time at Wander Creek or will she fall through the creek ice? You'll have to read this amazing book to find out. I'd highly recommend this book by the very talented author Amy Ruth Allen. **I look forward to the next book and all her books to come.**" – Reader

"**Another great read by Amy Ruth Allen. I thoroughly enjoyed reading this book and am looking forward to the next one in the series**. The main character, Abby is likable and all of her friends (and foes) are fun to get to know. The aura of mystery on who the benefactor is and who sabotaged her inventory keep you guessing until the very end. – Reader

PRAISE FOR AMY RUTH ALLEN

"I found the book Autumn on my kindle. The characters and the story were wonderfully written. It was a joy to read. I immediately purchased the book Spring and have read it in one evening. It also was wonderfully written. I have purchased the entire series with pre-order for Winter as it wasn't unavailable yet. With all that we are facing at this time in our country, these books take me away to another place for awhile. It was also fun to see that Amy Ruth Allen lives in my town Minneapolis, Minnesota."

— READER

"Felt like a good Hallmark movie. This was a sweet little book that felt like a good Hallmark movie. I liked the characters and the plot (except the sister). I was looking for an autumn themed book and this was a perfect choice. I can almost feel the autumn leaves rustling at Finch's Crossing."

— READER

"I have read Autumn and Spring back to back and have pre-ordered the next one due 1st August. I loved reading these books. Easy reading and feel good - especially good during the pandemic. I love that this series in set in a small village and everyone knows each other. Would recommend if you like easy reading and stories that wrap up eventually in each book."

— GOODREADS READER

"This was such a good book. I fell in love with the characters. Amy hit a homer with this!" –

— GOODREADS READER

"Oh I'd love to go on a vacation to Wander Creek. The great thing is I did while reading this book. This story is full of beautiful descriptions and wonderful, loving and caring characters. Including, a not so right in the head character that I love to hate. Through out this book you'll experience hard work, friendships, despair, worry, mystery, hardship, doubt, new beginnings and love. I absolutely enjoyed the wonderful writing from this very gifted author Amy Ruth Allen, and want everyone to experience this adventure throughout this marvelous book. I'm eager to know what's ahead for Abby, and can't wait for the next book!" –

— READER

"I thoroughly enjoyed reading this book and am looking forward to the next one in the series. The main character, Abby is likable and all of her friends (and foes) are fun to get to know. The aura of mystery on who the benefactor is and who sabotaged her inventory keep you guessing until the very end."

— READER

Made in the USA
Columbia, SC
03 December 2022

72599850R00102